Presents

Good Food

AN UNDERSTANDING OF BASIC ALCHEMY

The Daughters of Lilith Series

BOOK 3

Luna Charles

This fictional story's origin is purely that of the writer's imagination. Therefore, any characters, themes, and/or plots are coincidental. And should be regarded as such.

Warning:

The content of these novels is for pure entertainment and superfluous education. No item, herb, spell, or ritual in these books should be performed or ingested by anyone without the proper cleansing, overstanding, or supervision. Remember, all true wisdom comes from within and flows without. As above, so below; as within, so without.

Also, By Luna Charles

Men Are Not the Problem

- Vol I, II & III

My Life, My Rules

- Vol I & II

The Door – Short

The Healer's Persecution – Short

The Choices Made – Short

In the Beginning – Short

- Part of the Lilith Series

Good Food – BK 1

Good Food BK 2

Table of Contents

ASÉ

"A piece of gold that wants to shine must go through fire first." – *Yoruba Proverb*

Chapter XXXVI – *Oregano*

Oregano is a delicious herb found in most kitchen cabinets. It is rich in antioxidants and potent antibacterial, antifungal, and antiviral. It also helps fight cancer and decreases inflammation.

In Spiritual Work: *Oregano is feminine in energy. It is ruled by Venus and is considered an air element. Oregano can be used in spells involving luck, love, and happiness.*

It was Ceres's birthday night at the Bastille's beach house. Diana and Gerda had been on the couch, retrieving some loose obsidian stones from a small box of crystals, which Diana had inside her big chest of spiritual tools.

"Tonight," Diana confessed, "has me feeling unready."

"I know the feeling. Kids grow up so fast. I don't think we're ever ready as mothers."

"Yeah, but this is so much more," Diana was explaining the ritual she had performed with Ceres and Magalie on Friday. Gerda was family — a cousin on her mother's side — but her branch of the family had never been guardians of The Book, leaving her unfamiliar with such things.

Gerda had paused to ask Diana a question when, a moment later, everything went dark for Diana. She woke up to Gerda hovering over her.

"Diana, are you okay?"

"Ceres, I have to get to Ceres," Diana advised Gerda, who was helping her to her feet. Diana made it only a few feet from the couch before the darkness swallowed her and Gerda this time. When the two older women regained consciousness, they were unsure how much time had passed. They felt drained, as if they had been walking uphill all day, with sore muscles to prove it. Gerda and Diana were helping each other when they saw Ceres' glowing form walking out of the house towards the bonfire on the beach.

"Papa Bon Deux," Gerda gasped, crossing herself out of religious habits.

"Mother, protect us," Diana spoke softly. Whatever haziness remained cleared the moment she saw her daughter's state. She was too late.

In every *lwa*, like in the human Spirit, there are two sides. The polar opposite, we can call out or let us take over us, depending on our moods. The wolf, you feed, so to speak. At the moment, for reasons unknown to them, Ceres had been taken over by Erzulie Dantor, *Ge Rouge*, the young vengeful protector of women and children, revengeful of those who have wronged them. Red light streams trailed behind her as she walked, almost gliding toward the fire.

"Hurry, grab all the stones. We have to follow her." Diana spoke anxiously as she kept one eye on her oldest daughter moving quicker to get to the beach.

****

On the Beach, Leatrice rose to see what Magalie was looking at so fearfully towards the house. As soon as she saw Ceres, Leatrice took a step back in shock.

"Oh my God," Leatrice gasped.

Ceres' eyes were blank as she moved slowly to the fire, the Book firmly held against her chest. The two women watched as Ceres placed The

Book on the flat stone in front of the fire. Ceres stood still before the open Book, whose pages started flipping forward with an elegance that couldn't be caused by the wind.

Leatrice moved slowly toward the young Priestess. However, Magalie quickly waved her to remain where she was. As Magalie headed around the fire to face her sister.

"Cee," Magalie called out, but Ceres didn't make any movement that indicated she heard her sister as she remained blank in front of The Book.

"Ceres," Magalie spoke gently, taking a small step closer to her sister as she rubbed the protection ring on her hand.

Ceres slowly turned away from The Book, looking at Magalie with glowing green eyes empty of recognition, then turned back to The Book.

"Cee, snap out of it," Magalie spoke, a little louder this time, while she positioned her hands into fists by her sides, slipping her thumbs between her middle and index fingers.

It was a protective hand positioning that an old boyfriend had shown her years ago called a Kashyapa mudra: quick and simple energy protection, no fuss, no mess. Magalie didn't understand why she was mixing different practices at the moment. But her mother always told her that at the heart of them, all spirituality intersected with the spirit of God.

Pausing momentarily to breathe and center herself, Magalie took another step forward. This time, Ceres's whole body turned to face her younger sister, eyes still void of recognition. Magalie watched with curiosity as Ceres lifted her left hand slowly, palm facing out. For a moment, time slowed down. Magalie could see how Ceres' silver aura retracted from her whole body to form a single beam. Which shot out at Magalie, throwing her five feet across the sand.

****

To Magalie, the light hit like a wall of wind — she felt no fear until the sand came up to meet her. Then everything went dark.

Diana and Gerda arrived on the beach just in time to see Magalie get blasted away from Ceres by an energy beam that Diana didn't know was possible to create except in the movies. The color drained from her face as Diana watched Magalie land in the sand.

"Dear God," Both mothers spoke in unison as Diana shoved the stones in her hand at Gerda and then ran towards her youngest child.

"What the actual fuck?" Leatrice mouthed, frozen in shock, confusion, and fear, painting her features as she hurried towards Magalie.

Moments later, on the fire's far side, Magalie started to move.

"What the actual fuck is going on here?" The younger sister repeated as she coughed, brushing sand off as she rose to her feet just as Diana reached her.

"Mom, is there anything else you're not telling me about being a high Priestess? Like, maybe, X-Men-like powers?" Magalie asked as Diana finished her stand-up while keeping one eye on Ceres.

"No, Baby," Diana replied, brushing sand from Magalie's back as Leatrice reached them.

"Oh my God, are you okay?" Leatrice rambled as she reached Diana and Magalie.

"I'm good," Magalie advised.

"What is happening?" Leatrice asked, looking at Diana.

"I honestly don't know," Diana answered, her face as confused as Leatrice's.

A moment later, a breathless Gerda came running into the group of women staring at Ceres.

"What now?" Gerda asked.

Diana shook her head, her eyes not veering from Ceres, who still stood in front of the fire, looking possessed. Diana's mind had gone blank from shock.

"Mom, what do we do?" Magalie asked.

Diana didn't answer her daughter. As her eyes scanned around Ceres, trying to think of something. Finally, her eyes moved from Ceres toward the full moon. A beam of light seemed to flow from Ceres straight to the Moon.

'Diana, Goddess of the moon, my guardian and namesake, help me,' Diana thought, still staring at the Moon. From the West, the wind seemed to grow more robust, and a sudden calm came over the Matriarch with its touch. Closing her eyes, Diana took a deep breath and spoke.

"Holy Father, Divine Mother, allow me the aid of my guardian and teacher. I am lost."

There was only the sound of wind and crashing waves for a moment.

"The stones," came the voice of her higher self.

"Break the elemental union."

Suddenly, Diana understood what was happening and why she had been nudged to get the stones in the first place.

"Quick, the stones!" Diana shouted, jolting into action. "Start placing them in alternating colors of Clear Quartz and Black Onyx around Ceres in a wider circle, but leave an opening to the sea," Diana called out to Gerda, still not taking her eyes off her eldest.

As the group went into action, Ceres remained motionless and transfixed on the Book before her. She seemed utterly unaware of this world and everything happening around her. However, in front of Ceres, the pages of the Book had slowed down and then stopped at an unknown point.

Magalie and Leatrice were finishing working to the left of Ceres and instantly stopped when they heard the fluttering of pages halt.

"Holy shit," Magalie swore, her eyes wide as she saw the thin gossamer threads that seemed to flow from Ceres to the Moon grow thicker and brighter.

****

Leatrice, too, had become transfixed, her mind spinning.

"Mags," Diana screamed, breaking the spell, "finish the circle of protection you marked. Then step into it with Leatrice behind you and give Leatrice something to protect herself with."

"Mother, there is so much we need to discuss after this!" Magalie screamed, following Diana's commands but not taking her eyes off Ceres. "Like, really, what the fuck is happening with Ceres, is this part of the ritual we had on Friday?" Maggie shouted over the wind, unceremoniously grabbing the older woman's arm as she started pulling Leatrice into the new circle. The bewildered professor did not attempt to deter Magalie from moving closer to danger, even though she still gawked at Ceres' awe.

"Language," Diana shouted back.

"Sorry," Magalie replied, muttering something under her breath.

As Magalie walked Leatrice to her new position, she rummaged through her pockets for the black tourmaline and quartz crystal point pendant on a silver chain she always kept on her person. the youngest of them found the chain and placed it over Leatrice's head without asking her permission. The protective crystal pendant landed in the middle of her chest, right below her gold ankh. The chain seemed to break the hypnosis, and Leatrice regained her power of speech.

"Wait," holding on to the pendant, she bent over to breathe. "what is this?" Leatrice asked, trying to look at it as Magalie continued moving her toward the circle where Ceres was.

"Can we deal with this first?" Diana responded to Leatrice from the other side of the circle. She pulled an identical chain around her neck and placed it over Gerda's head.

"Stand behind me outside the circle here. You'll be safe. I'm moving off intuition here — just stay close and stay still, all right?" Diana directed Gerda to the south as she placed the last black stones inches from the water.

Quietly, Gerda nodded her understanding.

On Magalie's side, Leatrice had not responded to Diana and remained wild-eyed and fearful. So, Magalie paused and spoke firmly to the older woman. In a voice that any seasoned general would have listened to.

"Look, the pendant is tourmaline and quartz. Think of the two stones together as protection with a boost. I want you to hold on to it while you imagine a ball of white light forming around you, strong like *adamantium*, that nothing can break. Whatever you do, whatever happens, don't let go of that image, and stay outside the circle, behind me, where it's safe."

Leatrice mutely shook her head as she stood behind Magalie, the line of alternating-colored stones, and Ceres. Magalie removed the sterling silver ring with the hexagram engraving from her dominant right hand, the hand that sends energy out to the universe. To her left recessive hand, which takes in power from the universe. Changing the ring's job from shielding others to entirely focusing its protection on her.

As Magalie stepped over the threshold, she felt a wave of euphoric energy rush over, then heard an unfamiliar voice,

"*An extra pair of eyes to see, an extra vessel for the Lwa to speak through,*"

As the wave moved over her, the green flecks in Magalie's eyes joined to form a growing circle around her dark brown irises. Letting out a breath, Magalie fell to her knees in the sand.

"Magalie?" Leatrice called out, seeing the young woman fall.

When Magalie looked back at her while getting up, Leatrice gasped, her eyes widening as she tightened her grip around the pendant.

"Magalie, your eyes are glowing," Leatrice advised shakily.

Magalie smiled,

"It will be fine," she replied in a haunting voice as she moved around the circle to face her older sister from across the fire.

In front of Ceres, The Book's pages lay flat. Slowly, the young Priestess lifted her hands to the sky and sea, and the wind rose with her, scattering sparks of fire and sand.

"Hear me now, children of the light," Ceres' unearthly voice filled the air, unhindered by the wind.

When Diana stepped into the circle. She was still feeling unprepared. Until she was hit with the same euphoric energy that Magalie had encountered. She took a deep breath in as the green of her eyes encircled her brown irises. And a clearer understanding of what she had to do was imparted unto her. No one could go directly for Ceres while she was amid the four elements: air, water, fire, and earth. There would be more harm than good. Diana thought as she came to a stop next to Magalie.

However, when Magalie looked at her mother. Diana was shocked to see her daughter's glowing eyes.

"My God," Diana gasped.

Magalie smiled as if reading her mother's mind. She advised,

"Yours are glowing, too."

"Really?!" Diana reached up to see if she could see the reflection in her palm.

"Fire,"

It was as if Magalie was still reading her mother's thoughts. The fire was the only element they could take out of the equation. The bonfire was only a few feet from the ocean, but they could not move the water to kill it without leaving Ceres alone for too long, not knowing what she was up to. And Diana could not ask Gerda to put herself or Leatrice in an unknown danger by attacking the fire with water buckets.

"There has been enough innocent blood spilled," Ceres continued.

As Magalie stood watching and listening to her sister through the fire. Magalie felt like she was looking through someone else's eyes. As if she was a passenger observing someone else's actions and words as she rode safely and calmly in the back. With her face to the sea, Magalie stood straight up, arms stretched at her side. One palm faced up, while the other faced down, receiving energy and giving out power.

"In the name of The First daughter, the oldest Mambo, who is charged with protecting women, children, and intuition, Ayizan Velekete,

I invoke your name," Magalie called out, closing both hands with a clap.

Diana and Magalie stepped back as they felt a wave of energy from the clap rush past them. Diana's mind tried to recall the Deity's name. Magalie had just spoken.

'*The oldest of them,*' Diana's Spirit advised,

"Lilith's first daughter," Magalie replied without looking away from Ceres, still reading Diana's mind.

Around them, the sound and energy of the clap had increased tremendously. It fought to escape the circle of protection that had been put in place. Which only provided escape towards the ocean, where it was dissipated. At the water's edge, the wave of energy cascaded over Leatrice and Gerda with less force, thanks in part to their protective amulets. But still, with enough power to make them cover their ears from the sound.

Inside the circle, the wave's force had increased as the energy fed on itself. The small funnel provided for its escape was not releasing it fast enough. The vibration moved around the invisible barrier, looping counterclockwise, keeping Magalie and Diana unsteady.

"How much longer do you think she can keep this up?" Magalie asked her mother just as Diana stumbled.

Unsteadily, Magalie went over to Diana. A second later, Ceres lost her footing. And the pages of the Book started fluttering, too. Magalie smiled at what she could see from the corner of her eye. Clumsily, the two women got up, planting their feet in the sand. At the same time, Ceres regained her stance. For a moment, Ceres stared at the pages of The Book fluttered, no longer on the pages she was reading from. Then, Ceres stared at Magalie across the fire with glowing red eyes. Surprisingly, Magalie was staring back with a smile.

Slowly, Ceres lifted her hand over the Book. Magalie raised her hand towards Ceres, mirroring her sister's movement. Diana looked back and forth between her children, at a loss. When she had first entered the circle, Diana had been under the impression she was in charge of this plan. However, now, she saw this was between Ceres and Magalie. How Magalie, who had never really interacted with the Book as Ceres had, could call on one of the oldest Lwa astounded her. Diana saw her for what she must be: A Seer, there to help her sister carry her newly found power, see what Ceres could not in the hidden world, and control it.

The fire between them fluttered as the moon grew brighter while the two sisters faced each other. The three older women looked on with Gerda and Leatrice's hands holding firmly to their ears.

****

Leatrice had lost the grip that fears had over her and was now utterly enthralled by what she witnessed. In her wildest studies, Leatrice could never have imagined anything like this existing amongst black people in any century. Leatrice thought of St. George Church in Ethiopia and its miraculous construction. The young professor's mind was swarming with questions.

The wind rose higher inside the semicircle, battling against the three women. *'fire'* appeared brightly in Diana's mind before a sudden calm overcame her. Closing her eyes, Diana emptied her mind amid the chaos and spoke,

"In the name of the Holy Father and Divine Mother, Guardians, Teachers, and Guides. Aid me now. Work through me for our highest good."

'Water,' Diana heard her Spirit advise,

Diana's eyes flew open, and their glow seemed to increase. Diana slowly began walking backward toward Leatrice, Gerda, and the water as if in a trance. Diana didn't hear the women call out to her. She didn't feel the cold water rushing past her legs or her dress pulling heavy against them. She moved deeper, eyes wide open and not seeing.

Finally, Diana stopped when she was waist-deep in the water, aligned with Magalie and the fire. Then, lifting one palm facing upward to receive energy and one facing downward to give power, the mother of the young Priestess spoke,

"I call on the second daughter, teacher, and protector of my line, Goddess of the Ocean, Erzulie Dantor, to take my strength." Diana brought her hands together in a clap.

From where Gerda stood, the moonbeam appeared to split into three points, each dividing toward one of the three women embroiled in the battle. The wind rose higher at Diana's back as the water rushed around her waist in twin foaming waves towards the fire. Gerda saw the oncoming wave run past her friend faster than she could dig her feet deeper into the sand. The cold water overtook her, knocking Gerda off her feet and pulling her under.

****

Leatrice, however, had never taken her eyes off Diana since the woman passed them in a trance. The professor instantly saw the waters rushing towards her and positioned herself to go under the wave. Leatrice was about to go under herself when she saw Gerda get knocked down. Leatrice's heart sank because she knew her mother could not swim.

"Mom," Leatrice tried to scream as the water quickly filled her mouth, causing her to choke.

Spitting out the water, Leatrice dived back down and started swimming towards Gerda. Although Gerda always appeared brave by the ocean, Leatrice knew her mother had a deep phobia of drowning and had probably forgotten everything her daughter had taught her. In the dark, underneath the water, Leatrice felt her mother more than she saw her. A moment later, she wrapped her arms around Gerda's waist, pulling her upward.

The two women broke the surface, facing the fire. Gerda turned to place one arm around her daughter as she coughed up water.

"Are you okay?" Leatrice asked as they moved towards the beach.

Yes, Gerda nodded in affirmation as the two waves joined around Magalie and extinguished the fire with an instant whoosh. Sending a massive cloud of steam releasing grey-white vapors into the air. Everything seemed to happen quickly but also in slow motion. The triple beam from the moon and the cycle of wind died instantly with the fire. Causing the beach to become much darker and quieter than it had been. At that exact moment, Diana, Ceres, and Magalie fainted. Ceres and Magalie on either side of the bellowing steam. Diana fell unconsciously into the quickly receding water.

Gerda saw the two young women go down on the beach and turned around to check on her friend.

"Diana?" She screamed when she saw Diana floating on the water. Gerda tried to let go of her daughter.

"No, Mom. Go to the beach. I'll get her."

Gerda nodded, letting go, and started shakily through the lowering tide to the beach.

But before Leatrice took a step, Diana came to, screaming out,

"Yemoja,"

Gerda turned around and moved quickly to her friend. Giving up, Leatrice ran over to help Magalie, who was also waking up.

"Well, at least you can't say we're boring," Magalie chuckled as Leatrice put an arm around her waist.

"That's for sure," Leatrice laughed.

****

In front of them, Ceres was on her hands and knees, and Magalie could see that her sister's glow was still there but rapidly fading. Slowly, Leatrice and Magalie made their way to her.

Reaching the young Priestess as she shakily got to her feet.

"You're good, now?" the youngest asked, letting go of Leatrice to look her sister in the eyes.

"As above, so below, I see and understand," Ceres whispered, her eyes still looking far away.

Magalie sighed and rolled her eyes.

"Okay, so you're good," the younger sister replied sarcastically, placing her arm over Leatrice's shoulder again for support as she fished out her vape from her pocket, ensuring it wasn't wet.

The two wet mothers were walking up to the group just as Ceres picked up the undamaged Book from the makeshift altar. The whole group froze, with Diana and Magalie letting go of the women supporting them. However, the tension soon evaporated, and the women returned to their supporters. As Ceres simply held the Book to her chest and repeated to herself,

"I understand."

"You okay, Cee?" Diana asked with concern, soaked from head to toe, ambling as her friend supported her.

"I'll need more wine before she tells us about it." Magalie ascertained, finishing using the vape and offering it to Leatrice, who declined.

Chapter XXXVII - *Horsetail*

Horsetail weed or *Equisetum arvense* is a general antioxidant and is considered a super herb by some. Horsetail has been used for traditional remedies for urinary tract infections, healing bones, strengthening hair and teeth, and keeping the skin wrinkle-free. It also helps with arthritis (rheumatoid and osteo), osteoporosis, weak bladder, and chronic lung disease.

In Spiritual Work: *Horsetail is an herb of strength. Grow horsetail on your property to reinforce a boundary spell or add it to an enchantment to reaffirm commitment in a relationship. It can also be used for snake charming (not recommended) and fertility.*

"Fuck," Philia Coidavid swore, taking a deep breath while putting on her glasses. Then she started tapping on her phone screen to wake it up and looked at the time.

"Four a.m.," Philia complained loudly to no one as she rolled her eyes.

The top of her display was filled with notifications waiting for her attention. She sat up on the bed in a nightshirt and panties. Philia started sliding rapidly for deletion without bothering to see what they were about. The amount of social media notices Philia often received in one day for ARTS Tower was too much to go through thoroughly, even though it bothered her since she was meticulous. Almost done, Philia started getting up to brush her teeth and floss. When her finger stopped mid-slide.

Surprised, there was a message from her cousin Mateo. She sat back down and touched it. Philia's screen changed to the Facebook Messenger app. But under her cousin's face, the words *secret conversation* appeared with a timestamp of 18 hours ago. Philia looked at it in confusion as she pressed play on the first message. How could she have missed a Facebook message from her cousin yesterday?

"Phil, this first message is a test because I need you to pay close attention to the rest; each message will be deleted thirty seconds after you play it, and there is no replay."

The message ended, and a small timer followed the communication, counting down from thirty. Philia watched as the first message disappeared.

"Whoa."

Philia and Mateo had always been close, more siblings than cousins. Mateo treated her like he was her doting older brother. But when he took off, soon after his mother's death, to join a mission group overseas, he hadn't told her about it until the last day. She had been hurt but understood. He was close to his mom, and it had been him and her for a long time. Her uncle had always been too busy with business. Mateo's relationship with Jean, or lack of it, showed that.

He had been cryptic in the early part of his mission work, but their weekly phone calls remained constant. This kept Philia calm even when she couldn't tell her uncle she was in contact with Mateo. Her cousin had clarified that he didn't want Jean to know where he was but hadn't told her why. Then, last month, he called once to say he would be away from communication for a while. He had become paranoid that people were following him, but for her not to worry.

That day, a very worried Philia broke some rules. Without telling anyone, she accessed the Dieudonne family's satellite phone locator and discovered that Mateo had turned off his. Mateo had been serious when he said he didn't want anyone to find him. The last place he was pinned was somewhere in East Africa, which wasn't surprising since he was supposed to be in Somalia. And now this; these messages.

Pulling off the floral print scarf to scratch her head, Philia was just about to push play on the following message when she remembered the instructions from the first. Searching through the drawer of her nightstand, she found a pen and a notebook she had for just such circumstances. Written notes had never failed her when dealing with the Dieudonne men. Placing everything at the ready, Philia pushed play on the following message. Mateo's voice wasn't the calm, soothing voice she was used to. Instead, his words carried a sense of urgency.

"*Ti Soeur, so much has happened since we last spoke that I don't know where to begin. Since I'm still piecing things together. But I need you to believe me right now.*" He paused, taking a breath.

"*Last time we spoke, I told you I would be away for a while but didn't tell you why. Over the past month, I've had some kids from Kenya volunteer with me. One of them was an up-and-coming documentarian, Imanau. He and I have become very close during our travels, bonding through blood, as they say.*

Imanau and I had been in Somalia for a couple of weeks when a group of doctors we were not familiar with came into the camp suddenly. They asked for blood samples from all the Americans and Europeans to run a test. I'm not even sure," he paused.

"The doctor that took my blood, I was sure I had met before. At least, I had seen him before, with my father. Phili, this man's face, wasn't the kind of face you forgot. *comprenez vous?* With albino white skin and yellow eyes. Even hidden under the doctor's mask, he stood out. I was so shaken that Imanau thought it would be helpful to leave the area.

He had been planning a trip to the City of Lalibela, a Northern Ethiopian city famous for the monolithic buildings carved out of solid rock. For the project he was working on titled *The History and the Stolen Wealth of the African People*, I went with him. Soeur, things just got weirder there," He laughed a little sarcastically, "My mother always said you cannot run from your path,"

Philia was bent over the phone, listening to her cousin intently, constantly touching the screen so it would not go off. She didn't know what exactly to make of what Mateo was saying.

"We were at Lalibela, visiting The Church of Saint George. I was leaning over the edge of the circular pit. Which had been dug into the earth to reveal the even-length cross-shaped, four-story building. Our family's crest pendant had been hanging from my shirt, shining in a photographer's eyes. He was surprised and disconcerted that a European was wearing it. Which led to a long conversation about our family crest and my mother's Moorish ancestry. Mateo started sounding more serious,

"He told me there was a place I might find answers if I could find my way in because outsiders were not allowed in Benin.

The photographer said our crest was an exact duplicate of the most sacred of them. He told me the story of the symbol on the back of our family Book, the striped diamond with the four overextended arms and six stars around it, representing Ayizan, the Teacher. Legend says she came from the north and knew the secrets of the hidden world, with excellent knowledge of the connections between humanity and the divine that could be used for great wealth and control. When she left her temple, they took four Handmaidens to teach them about nature and gifts.

The people in the village supposedly have an oral and written history of these powerful iconographies they use in their religious practices to bring health, wealth, insight, and protection, dating back thousands of years. They say their powers were stolen during the slave trade and reused unethically by white masters. So elite families gave these magical sigils to add *to their coat of arms to gain power and wealth."* Mateo paused again, catching his breath. In the background, it sounded like children were playing in a language foreign to Philia, as a soft horn could be heard blowing behind him.

The message ended, and the little timer appeared.

Benin, Philia thought. Something was nagging her.

Why and how did a French family's crest end up in a country in West Africa? She slowed down her train of thought, closing her eyes.

Philia imagined The Dieudonne corporate logo. She had been around it every day for years at the office, picturing it easily. It did feature three interlocking circles signifying Jean, Esperanza, and Mateo for as long as Philia could remember. The logo was inside a diamond for the four corners of the world. Her mind stretched.

A flash of memory interrupted Philia's thoughts. It was the cover of the family's Book. Philia remembered Esperanza telling her Jean used the artwork for the corporate logo because it was *lucky*. The Book was an heirloom passed down from generation to generation of firstborn daughters. Philia's mom once believed Esperanza would give The Book to her since Esperanza only had a boy, but that never happened before Esperanza passed.

It had been years since she saw it, and she was surprised by how clearly she remembered the cover. The striped diamond with the four overextended arms and six stars around it finished the design. Jean changed it to make it simpler, more appealing to the masses, and easier to recognize.

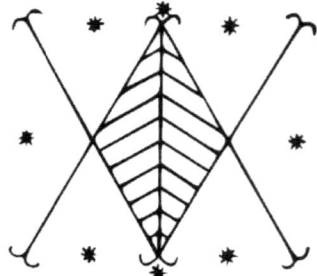

But something else in her brain was itching to be scratched. Like there was more wanting to reveal itself, a thin layer of mental fog prevented it. A gut feeling told Philia that he would find the original one, not the 2.0 version, whenever Mateo finally found that village. Her mother and aunt were Spanish, from Andalusia, Spain. A place in the South of Spain was called Muslim Spain because it was once ruled by the Moors. Their great-grandmother's maiden name was Anum, Egyptian. Mateo told Philia he wanted to learn more about The Great Library. Still, even with those connections, that was far from Benin.

Philia frowned. The pieces weren't coming together as fast as she had. All her life, Philia had the uncanny ability to put things together. It wasn't problem-solving per se. Instead, she could see the invisible connections stretching forward and backward.

She thought people came to Egypt from everywhere as she pushed play on the following message.

"Philia, if it's one thing I learned from my mother's lessons, nothing can be obtained for free. Blood was spilled by these families to get their wealth. And I think my mother, her sickness, and her unborn children were the sacrifices for our wealth," Mateo choked up on the other end, coughing to clear his throat,

"*Before my mother died, she told me, the reason for her sickness and that she couldn't have more children was that they had used sacred knowledge to selfishly attain wealth. She tried to convince my dad that her ailments were outside western medicine, which is why western medicine couldn't help. But my father insisted that western medicine was lacking, calling her paranoid when she accused him of using what she called 'knowledge unspeakable by his kind' to save her life the wrong way.*

My father went on trips during this time and wouldn't tell us about them. And when he came back, he was constantly hovering over her, bringing different things—potions, herbs, charms, he thought could help. Finally, after one of those trips, I saw him with the albino man in the library. My mother was sick in her bed, and my dad didn't know I was home. They were whispering over the family Book. I could tell my father was upset. The only thing I could make out was, 'I should be able to read it by now.'

Phili, I'm honestly at a loss right now. I don't know what to think or how everything is connected. And maybe I'm paranoid to believe this was the same man Because why would he follow me to Africa? Like my mother and me, you can read the Family's Book. You've done it before with my mom. I need you to get a hold of it," Mateo paused,

"Holy Batman," Philia swore, pulling off her glasses to clean them with her shirt.

As Mateo spoke, Philia's mind was spinning. She couldn't believe what she was hearing.

Philia sat for a moment, totally at a loss, her hands shaking.

What was Mateo saying?

Chapter XXXVIII – *Wolfsbane*

Poisonous Wolfbane is acclaimed in traditional herbal medicine due to its healing actions, which were considered analgesic, anti-rheumatic, sedative, fever-reducing, and anti-inflammatory. Wolfsbane is included in the treatment of joint and muscle pain. Also claimed that applying it to the skin slows the heart rate in cardiac patients.

In Spiritual Work: *Cited it as a protective plant. It's beneficial for invoking Hecate, The Goddess of the Moon. It could be used in sympathetic magic to harm another by creating "elf bolts" of sharpened flint dipped in wolfsbane juice and piercing a poppet for the victim with them.*

Jean told Philia of the paranoia that had gripped Esperanza in the last moments of her life. Now, her cousin sounded like he was becoming equally paranoid. After not hearing from him for a month, Philia wondered if anything else had happened that was making him say these things.

His words made Philia feel sick to her stomach. How could he possibly think the money his father had made as an intuitive businessman was the cause of his mother's cancer? Philia had no doubt Jean loved Esperanza and his family. However, nothing Mateo was saying made sense. Sure, there were rumors, but aren't stories commonplace regarding how influential people attain their wealth? Weren't rappers, as well as oil tycoons, accused of being members of the Illuminati? Philia took a deep breath, rubbing her loose hair feverishly before hesitantly pushing play on the third message.

Mateo continued,

"Hey, I've been in Benin now for half a day. I don't know if you got my last message, but we came here to access the village. However, when I woke up this morning, Imanau was gone. He left me a note asking me to meet him at this cafe. But when I arrived, no one knew what I was talking about. I'm hoping I missed my ride, so I've been speaking to the locals. At least the ones that will talk to me about the place. I have no idea where it's located, except it's high in the

mountains near a large river," Mateo paused and started to shout at someone to wait on him in French,

"Phil, I've got to go. Please go to the beach house in Fort Pierce when you can. I'll call you as soon as I'm able. I need you to look for something in The Book for me. I think you, of all people, can help finish putting together this puzzle. I need to know if our family has possession of stolen ancient African Magic. Through The Book that has brought our family great wealth but also cursed us, Ti Soeur. I hope I'm wrong,"

The message ended. The timer came up.

Philia wrote her thoughts as fast as she could on a paper pad. She needed to know who Ayizan, The Teacher, was and how their family was connected to Benin. And what else? She felt uneasy inside, as she said out loud,

"If my uncle has been using our families for wealth that cursed us?" She thought about how her mother and aunt died from cancer, one only a few months after the other. When there was no trace in their bloodline before.

Philia knew her cousin, Mateo, was a bit of a conspiracy theorist, and she was too. Yet, she had to admit her uncle had been acting odd for a while now. She had been on a rollercoaster ride with him while Mateo was out chasing myths.

"Benin," she shouted, switching on her light and leaving. Where had the Teacher come from, and where did she go? But, first, she had to get to Fort Pierce and look at The Book again.

"Fuck!" Philia moaned, remembering that her uncle thought The Book was gone.

Her stomach turned with anxiety. Philia had never told such a big lie to anyone in her life. Well, technically, she reasoned, it wasn't a lie. So, she didn't say anything when she overheard Shaka and her uncle speaking about the missing Book in his office. Jean thought The Book was lost or had been stolen right after Esperanza's funeral, but Philia had a mercurial memory of Mateo carrying it out of the house sometime after that. They were at home in Fort Pierce. It was a few days before Mateo left for Somalia. So, when her uncle said it was gone, she assumed Mateo just hid it from him for some reason before he left; that size book wasn't something you carried when you needed to move fast and light. And since he was telling her to go look through it for clues, her assumptions were proving to be correct.

Philia reasoned Mateo had the right to withhold The Book from his father if he wanted to. After all, it was his mother's Book; maybe he wanted to keep that piece of hers for himself. That wasn't hard to believe given the history of animosity between her cousin and his father over the years, which only grew since Esperanza's passing. Now Philia was starting to think it was for entirely different reasons. The problem was locating The Book if Mateo did hide it there. How would she find something Jean couldn't find in his own house?

Philia was sure of one thing: something would be revealed in Fort Pierce. The women in their family didn't believe in coincidences. Synchronicity was more of their thing. So, it was no coincidence that her uncle invited her to Fort Pierce hours before her cousin told her to go there. And two, Philia knew she had to take immediate action. Philia remembered the law of motion her aunt had taught her: whenever you're searching for something, as long as you keep your thoughts on it while taking action. Your feet would lead you to where you needed to go. Either way, she was meant to be in Fort Pierce today and needed to move fast.

Philia glanced at her watch. It was just now turning a quarter past five. She estimated by the time she got ready and figured out what she was buying for breakfast, the pilot would be up and about.

"If I was Mateo, where would I hide The Book?" Philia was questioning herself as she walked around the apartment, getting ready.

She pulled out an overnight suitcase from the side of her walk-in closet that Mia Toro decorated with colorful butterflies. She placed it on the bed to pack.

"If I was Mateo, where would I hide The Book?" She asked herself again, standing at the dresser, looking through her undergarments to match panties and bras.

Philia froze as something clicked. They were younger; Mateo was hiding The Book from his dad. She didn't remember why he was doing that, but his mom was sick, and Jean and Mateo were fighting, as usual. Mateo had taken Philia into his room, sitting her on the bed while he packed. As Mateo rambled about his disagreement with his father, he pushed the start button on something that looked like an Xbox video game console, but instead, the box opened like a shell to reveal The Book inside. Philia had remarked that it was an excellent hiding place.

"My dad would never imagine something like this was possible," Philia repeated, quoting Mateo's words. She snapped her fingers as a triumphant look brightened her face.

The Book must still be there, Philia decided. Mateo must have left it at the house after his mother passed away before he went to Africa. She was confident that this train of thought was correct. Philia headed to the bathroom to get ready. Then, with a deep breath, she repeated the invocation of her ancestors to start this journey.

"May the God who created me take my hand, direct the breath of my mouth, and lead my feet where I may manifest my birthright."

This, Philia felt, would be a mystery that could help her answer some questions haunting her.

Chapter XXXIX – *Chestnuts*

Chestnuts remain a good source of antioxidants, even after cooking. They're rich in gallic acid and ellagic acid—two antioxidants that increase in concentration when cooked. Antioxidants and minerals like magnesium and potassium help reduce your risk of cardiovascular issues, such as heart disease or stroke.

In Spiritual Work: *Chestnuts can be eaten to encourage fertility and desire and may be carried as a charm by women who wish to conceive. Keeping chestnuts around the house (and eating them) encourages abundance.*

"Philia is not with her uncle," Ahkter spoke softly as his brother half-carried him into the room. Ahkter's energy had been severely drained from the cloaking spell at the restaurant earlier.

"She will be in the office early tomorrow morning,"

"Yes," Mahkter confirmed, finishing his brother's thoughts as he laid him down on one of the two queen beds, "We will rest for a few hours, then meet her before she goes inside the office building,"

The following morning, Ahkter woke to sunlight streaming through thin curtains — his energy so depleted that for a moment he couldn't remember where he was or why. Ahkter slowly sat up, inching forward until he sat on the bed's edge. Mahkter woke up next with a start, as groggy and confused as his brother, but with eyes wide open to the harsh sun.

"Merda!" He swore quickly, closing his eyes.

"You shouldn't swear," Ahkter warned him softly as his mind began to congeal. Then, standing up slowly, still weak from the spell last night. He walked over to the bright window, searched the curtain's edge until he found the pole, and pulled shut the room's darkening curtains.

As the brothers' memories returned to them, neither man recalled suddenly sitting up in bed last night, a little past 11:30, to speak one sentence.

"Les étoiles sont alignées," *the stars are aligned.*

By the time Ahkter made it back to the bed, Mahkter was fully awake, calling the pilot to verify what airport he was at, moving on to plan B without a pause. Ahkter looked down at his watch and groaned when he realized it was already 8:30.

"I have never woken up past dawn," he complained.

"And we've never been this old and used so much energy. It's time for us to retake the elixir," Mahkter advised.

"No, not yet. We have to have the girl first. We can't afford to take a week away to recover from the process with everything happening now. I'll take some tonic on the plane,"

"Agreed, the plane is in hangar 11 at APP Jet Center, 15 mins away without traffic. If we hurry, we can catch her when she leaves the building for lunch," Mahkter advised as he helped his brother up and started their way out of the hotel,

"And we can shower and change before landing," Ahkter offered.

"Jesus, yes! I can't believe I've been wearing the suit for two days," Mahkter complained.

"Three," Ahkter corrected, "don't swear,"

Ten minutes later, the twins believed their lives were the outcome of a series of moments God created. The men, who knew with absolution, the sun rose and set, the world went around, and everything that happened per God's timing and planning, were trying to figure out why, as sacred soldiers of God, God's plans seem to be keeping the twins from serving The Eternal?

The men were only 7 minutes away from the hangar when an apparent car crash somewhere in front of them brought I-95 to a standstill. At the time, the twins were driving in the far-left lane, and since they were new to the area, they depended heavily on their GPS to direct them to their goal. Therefore, the brothers found themselves stuck between exits, trapped on a 3-mi-long stretch of highway.

The sun seemed brighter than ever, with every ray of sunlight penetrating through the dark tints, draining their energy. Ahkter had reclined his seat entirely back to the point he was almost lying down in the passenger seat, with the sun only touching his lap. At the same time, Mahkter, sporting a new pair of aviator sunglasses he had bought on their way out of the hotel, was trying to stay focused on getting them to the hangar and into the safe comfort of the jet.

"Do you ever think that The Father is keeping us away from them? Away from the knowledge we seek?" Mahkter asked softly.

"Don't blaspheme," his brother replied, adjusting himself in the seat to look at his younger sibling, "The powers of evil always put up a greater fight when there's more for it to gain. Our Father will only help us as much as we help ourselves. We know if our will is strong enough, so it shall be,"

"Of course, you're right," Mahkter agreed as he looked down at his brother.

Mahkter might have seen the Light Blue Bel Air if he hadn't turned around. It exited ahead, taking a local back street to the other side of the executive airport. Instead, when Mahkter looked up again, he could only observe the bright reflective sunlight on the rear windshields of the cars around him.

"Merda," He groaned at the sight.

Twenty minutes later, the brothers finally made it off the exit. They arrived at the hangar just before Mahkter saw the Bombardier with Jean's company logo on the tail taxiing down the runway.

"Is that Jean's jet," Mahkter asked dumbfounded, staring upward at the tail, sure that it was the logo but hoping he was wrong.

"Yes," Ahkter confirmed with a groan, looking at it as he sat up, "he is probably heading back to Tallahassee, to Philia,"

"What now?"

"We follow. There will be a point when Philia is alone and vulnerable. We can't go back home without answers. Not when we're so close."

Chapter XL -*Dragon Fruit*

Dragon fruit contains high amounts of fiber that maintain blood sugar levels and avoid spikes among people suffering from diabetes. It helps reduce the risks of Cancer, helps boost immunity, and is suitable for digestion.

In Spiritual Work: *Eat dragon fruit to connect to the moon, open your sacral chakra, and increase creativity while working with the dragon spirit guide.*

Leatrice had spent hours scanning The Book, feverishly searching for information about its origin. Then, sometime during the pre-dawn hours, Leatrice figured out she could read the manuscript better when she was close to one of the Bastille girls. And had been shadowing one of them around the house with the large Book in hand.

Now, with the sun fully risen over the soft blue horizon, Leatrice read as quietly as possible on the couch while Magalie meditated in the lotus position in front of her. She hoped to discover some systematic route through the information scrawled on the pages.

Leatrice wasn't sure what she was looking for. At first, she hoped to discover a time frame in the B.C. era that would allow her to put the information in chronological order. Yet, there were no dates in any particular sequence; while one page would reference 2000 B.C., the next would be a different writing style from 1000 B.C. Soon, Leatrice realized that her initial plan was not going to work.

The more she tried to make sense of it, the more The Book revealed it had no end to its depth of knowledge. Also, there was no order to it either. Instead, the information seemed to show what was aligned with the reader's thinking, from page to page, like a fortune teller's crystal ball. The first time she became aware of it, Leatrice had been distracted by a particular herb she saw in the kitchen while Ceres was making tea. Before Leatrice had a chance to ask, the medical and metaphysical uses for the plant appeared on the page — when nothing about it had been there a moment before. The second time, Maggie commented on moon phases and plant growth. The information on that topic also presented itself on the page in front of Leatrice.

This caused Leatrice to conclude that the depth and abundance of information in The Book could never be read in exact order and that The Book worked in a symbiotic relationship with the reader by providing the precise information they needed without wasting time searching for it. So, although Leatrice could read The Book, she knew it was a simple matter. She was sure she would never be able to read the hidden layers like the Bastille women could.

'Everything happens for a reason,' Leatrice heard the other voice in her head say.

The words echoed in her mind as she attempted to breathe calmly and methodically, knowing her inner voice reminded her to relax and let go of the anxiety she felt growing within herself. The knot had grown to the point Leatrice had never experienced before after Diana called the house from the chiropractor's office. She informed Leatrice that she had accidentally taken her phone by mistake. And Jean Dieudonne had called several times, leaving messages. That was when Leatrice remembered she had the page from his Book. She quickly retrieved it from the car for the sister to examine. Still, even with the Bastille women touching it, the sheet only continued to reveal the same two lines.

les étoiles se sont alignées. Ton temps est maintenant. The stars are aligned. Your time is now.

Aware of Lilith's deal, the ladies pondered what was meant by 'the time is now? Were they in the midst of the shift, or was it impending? They had left the page in the folder on the kitchen counter.

"Everything will work out how it's supposed to," comforted Ceres, rubbing Leatrice's shoulder.

She left in a t-shirt and jeans to the family's spice and tea shop for ingredients like adder's tongue bluebells, marjoram, and licorice root. While her mother went upstairs to take a much-needed nap. Magalie calmly meditated in front of her in red and black flannel pajama pants and a white t-shirt. Proceeding with their day as if movie-worthy supernatural events hadn't happened a few hours ago. Leatrice, though, try as she might, could not slow down the pounding in her chest from nervousness.

The Young doctor put down The Book to clear her head, looking towards the water. In the distance, a gathering of dark clouds mirrored the internal turmoil in her Spirit. So much had happened and was going on in her mind. Leatrice just didn't know how to sort anything out. She shared the same bloodline as Lilith, supposedly Adam's first wife, which was never discussed in church.

Now, with everything the young professor had witnessed, she felt embarrassed that she had used a lackadaisical excuse to stop following what her gut instincts had tried to push her towards.

"By the pricking of my thumb," Magalie commented, suddenly stretching out of her meditation.

"Something wicked this way comes." Leatrice finished the line from *Macbeth*. As if on cue, the alarm on the front door beeped, letting the women inside know someone had opened it.

"Ceres?" Magalie called out.

"Yeah, what's up?"

"Nothing. You brought something wicked?" Magalie lowered her voice as her sister walked into the kitchen. Leatrice was laughing until she saw the crafty look on Ceres' face.

"What would you consider wicked?" Ceres asked her sister.

Magalie and Leatrice moved to the kitchen.

"Where's Gerda?" Ceres questioned.

"Upstairs. Mom had a headache, so she went to lie down in the guest bedroom," answered

Leatrice while pulling things out of the bags and placing them on the counter.

"More wine!" Magalie said excitedly as she started to unpack the bags in front of her as if she had just scored a win.

"You're going to be drunk by the time it's legal for you to drink," Ceres jokes.

"I'm legal in France," Magalie shouted, sticking her tongue out at her sister.

Ceres quickly moved around Leatrice, grabbing the bottles of red wine from the paper bag in front of her sister.

"It's not all for us," Ceres informed Magalie, placing a couple bottles in the sink. "While I was at the store, I had an idea," she continued with a smile.

"Something wicked?" Magalie confirmed, causing Leatrice to chuckle, easing her nervousness.

"Maybe," Ceres answered honestly. "Mags, do you remember John's party?"

"How could anyone forget? John was this guy that was dating Ceres and...."

"We were not dating."

"Yea, yea. So, John is dating Ceres; Dax, her best friend, starts talking about this guy named John. That she had met at the shooting range, who she went out on a date with,"

"It didn't take us long to figure out. We were talking about the same, blonde-haired, blue-eyed, All-American boy from Ohio that liked to bodyboard," Ceres added, sucking her teeth as she interrupted again.

"So," Magalie started again but stopped when her sister continued.

"When I asked John while we were out if he was dating anyone else, and he said no, I was pissed."

"Super pissed," Magalie added.

"I was young then and easily given to my emotions,"

"It was two years ago," Magalie replied, laughing as she popped a grape into her mouth.

"Exactly!" Ceres exclaimed. "That's a lifetime in personal growth for a woman,"

"Wait, weren't you in class two years ago?" Leatrice asked as the timeframe became clear to her.

"Yep."

"I had John, a white kid. He dropped out in the middle of the semester after he confessed to all his teachers that he had been cheating by buying papers online if I remember correctly,"

Ceres and Magalie busted out laughing, forcing Leatrice to stop talking.

"What did you do to him?" Leatrice asked Ceres, her face alive with excitement.

"Nothing much; He just developed a need to be more honest with others. At least for a little while," Ceres finished with a wink.

"After drinking a specially made sangria," Magalie confirmed, handing Leatrice a bottle labeled Bluebell Tincture.

Leatrice could not help laughing herself.

"You can do that?"

"We all can," Magalie answered, sitting at the kitchen bar. "Getting someone, to tell the truth, using herbs is no more amazing than smoking weed to get high or drinking ginger for an upset stomach. It's all in the knowledge of the plants. I've learned that nature will provide for the sick, unbeknownst to them. All people have to do is look in their backyard. The remedy for what ails them is probably there."

Ceres and Leatrice looked at the youngest of them. She had spoken as if she was much older than her years. For a second, an older woman in white appeared to be standing behind her.

"Ayizan," Ceres whispered at the vision.

The older woman looked at her and vanished, leaving Magalie nodding her head to the truth of her words.

"What did you say?" Leatrice asked, looking at Ceres.

"Nothing. I thought I saw...."

"Me too, but what was the name you said?"

"You too, what?" asked Magalie, looking at the women across from her.

"Ayizan," Ceres spoke softly to her sister, "The eldest daughter,"

****

At her words, the apparition reappeared, causing Leatrice's heart to increase in palpitation. Then, as Magalie felt a slight pressure on her shoulder, the young woman hesitantly turned to face it. Yet she was not fearful when she faced the tall, dark woman, wearing thin white fabric layered on each other, resembling a one-shoulder toga and a jumpsuit mixture.

The bottom of her face was veiled. The veil was secured by a silver tiara on top of her dreadlocked hair. The hair was grey at the crown and darkened towards the end. Her outfit flowed to the floor, but she did not touch it. Instead, it seemed to hover above it. She was adorned in silver jewelry with bracelets stacked three on each arm.

Magalie reflexively pulled back from her before the apparition looked deep into the little girl's eyes, and the woman's hypnotic gaze calmly froze her.

"See, Er," she whispered to Magalie, stepping forward and kissing Magalie's forehead.

"Ayizan, *pale a pitit ou,*" Ceres reached out to her, begging her to stay and speak to them. But she vanished with the kiss.

"Okay, so I just see that?" Leatrice questioned nervously, "This is really happening," she commented, trying to breathe calmly.

The sound of Gerda descending the stairs cut her off and caused all the women to jump with nervousness.

"What did I just catch you guys doing?"

"Oh, nothing, just visiting with things that vanish before our eyes," Leatrice chuckled skittishly.

"And here I thought all the action happened last night," Gerda sucked her teeth before kissing her daughter on the cheek and looking at Ceres questioningly. Ceres, in turn, looked at Magalie.

"Okay, so the thing is," Magalie started after a while, "I don't think I'm a Seer. I think when I'm balancing out the flow of energy to you. If that's what we want to call it. I received the information on how to do it from her."

"Ayizan?"

Chapter XLI - *Sage*

Sage or salvia is a prevalent herb found in millions of kitchens. As a tea, it will help settle a sour stomach and ease digestion. In addition, it's rich in antioxidants, great for oral health, alleviates menopause symptoms, helps fight diabetes, and helps with memory loss.

In Spiritual Work: *It is mainly used as a magical herb for protection and purification. But sage can be used in magical workings for immortality, longevity, wisdom, and granting wishes.*

At 6:00 in the morning, fully packed and unable to stay still, Philia drove to ARTS tower to ensure her out-of-office assistant was set up for her and Jean, and to leave a note for the secretary to forward only the most important calls. Philia understood she could have done all of this over the phone. She was reluctant to admit that she had been looking for clues in her uncle's office. Which caused her to arrive late to meet their pilot, Jesus, at the airport. Jesus was Brazilian by birth, raised in Miami by his own account — as American as apple pie, except with a year-round tan. The tall, athletic, dark-haired man had an easy smile that made passengers feel better about being airborne.

It was 8:45 a.m. when the bombardier landed at the APP Jet Center in Fort Pierce and taxied to a stop in hangar 11. Philia was feeling a little drunk but calmer than before. At the suggestion of Jesus, she took three shots of vodka as soon as she got on the plane to calm her nerves. Philia hated flying, not born into the jet-set lifestyle as the daughter of a bookshop owner. Nonetheless, she was pleased that she at least could dress the part, taking comfort in her sharp, classic black Alexander McQueen suit and cute Coach loafers.

The pilot walked up to her seat with a grin.

"Ms. Philia, you're safe now. I told you you would be okay with Jesus at the wheel,"

Philia looked up at him with a wry smile, standing up to get ready to leave, and almost lost her balance as the world tilted around her. However, she quickly grabbed the back of the cream-colored chair to stabilize herself.

"Are you all right?" Jesus asked, offering his hand to her.

She chuckled, still feeling a bit woozy,

"I'm fine. It's a good thing I'm not driving, though," Philia giggled, taking Jesus' hand as he gathered Philia's messenger bag on the seat in front of her.

"Will I be leaving with the car to Tallahassee right away?" He asked, opening the jet door to let her down the stairs and help her with her things.

"I honestly don't think so. I'm not sure how long my uncle will be here, but he'll want to drive that car around. Why don't you take the plane to Miami and visit your Abuela for the day until I have better information?" She offered at the foot of the stairs as he placed her butterfly suitcase down.

"Sounds good. I can use a good breakfast,"

Philia shook with a chuckle,

"Men, food, and sex, that's it,"

"Aye, Ms., what can I say? We're simple creatures," Jesus affirmed with a smile, kissing her on the cheek, "You call, and I'll come,"

"Sim, I know I can always rely on Jesus to be there right on time," She laughed, using one of his puns, causing the pilot to chuckle back into the plane.

Standing on the ground in the hangar, Jesus closed the door behind her. Philia was surprised they were in a shared hangar beside a Gulfstream G650.

"Yes," she commented with a victory fist as she swung the messenger bag carrying the laptop over her shoulder.

Philia wondered if the pilot or the owner was nearby. Maybe she could get a tour. She felt a strange attachment to the plane, a pull as if it were calling her.

"Because we are supposed to be together," Philia said aloud with a smile.

However, the smile quickly faded when the young woman thought she heard her aunt's voice. Pausing a few feet from the tail to listen as the last echoes of her footsteps faded,

'*Phil*,' the whisper came again, so close she turned to see, but no one was there.

"Hello?"

But no answer came,

Great, she thought, *just three shots, and I hear things: lightweight.*

Shaking her head in disapproval of herself, Philia started back toward the tail of the plane.

When the sound of a car pulling up to the hanger caught her attention, Philia took a few steps back to look out of the bay doors.

The baby-blue Bel-Air had just stopped in front of the hanger. As Shaka and her uncle exited — both dressed like they were headed to a vacation rather than a meeting — Philia started walking toward them. However, their clothes were a sharp contrast to her attire. Her uncle wore cargo pants, a cream-collared shirt, and a hat, looking like he was going on a safari. While Shaka was in blue jeans and a Hawaiian shirt. Philia tried to hold in a snicker as she saw the odd attire on the large man. Even though it worked for him, it was not something a man of his complexion and size could easily pull off. They looked like they had been dressed for a Magazine's Miami-style issue.

Philia was all smiles, waving to them as she went to get her bag. Her stomach turned as anxiety spread as soon as she remembered this was not a vacation. Her cousin had given her a mission. Smiling weakly as Shaka ran over to get her bag, she kissed the big man on the cheek.

"Hey, you, okay?" He asked, towering over with a concerned look.

"Yeah, I'm great," She tried to brighten her voice, "You know, me and flying aren't the best of friends," she explained, taking a deep breath.

Today, she reminded herself, she had to lie better than she ever had before.

Jean was waving to Jesus, who was already back in the cockpit.

"I told him to take the plane to visit his Abuela, and we will call him when we are ready," She shouted to her uncle.

"Good, I'm sorry we're late, there was an accident, and we 're stuck in traffic." He confessed, reaching up to them and kissing her on both cheeks, "Are you ready? I'm starving,"

For a second, Philia thought she would burst into tears looking into the gentle blue eyes of her uncle. She could not imagine any of the things that his son was saying could be true. How could this sweet old man have let his wife, the woman he loved, die for money? All her uncle wanted to do was make people happy and eat. Swallowing hard, Philia found the strength to hug him tightly without spilling a tear. Yet, she could not deny what she knew; she had done some research before landing.

"Yes, Tonton, I made a reservation not too far," She managed to get out with a forced smile as they started walking back toward the car.

So far, Philia has learned that Ayizan was a form of deity from the Yoruba religion of West Africa. A being known for wisdom, protecting women, children, and the marketplace. Connecting humanity with the Divine and keeping the peace. Moreover, she gave her followers great gifts of fine wine and clothing.

Still, Philia felt there was more to be learned about Ayizan, which seemed harder to find than it should be in this age of Google.

She had many questions: what did her family Book have to do with Yoruba? They were a Catholic family. Her patron saint was St. Claire of Assisi. She even had her first communion, the Onyx Rosary, around her neck because it made her feel safe while flying.

"Deep thoughts?" Shaka asked, walking up to her.

Philia was startled to find she was standing in front of the car. The young woman walked the whole way in a fog.

"Oh no," She answered. As Shaka opened the truck to put her bag in it,

"Where is breakfast?" Jean asked, opening the back passenger door to let her in.

"I have a reservation at a place 10 minutes from here, voted best-stuffed crepes in Florida." Philia was used to anticipating her uncle's needs. Jean's face brightened for a few seconds before sadness darkened it.

"It will never be as good as your *Tante's*," he said softly, getting in the passenger side as Philia got into the backseat and touched his shoulder. Jean reached back and squeezed it.

Driving away, Philia looked back to see Jesus taxiing the Bombardier from the hangar toward the runway. As a black SUV approached the bay doors, the sun shone brightly against its windshield.

Damn, the young woman thought, *a few more minutes, and I could have met the owners and maybe gotten a tour.*

The traffic must have cleared up when they got back on the road—the drive down only took the trio ten minutes. Riding down the coast in the convertible was everything Philia needed to settle her mind from her recent flying fears.

"One, they go with the suit. And two, I wanted to look fancy getting off the jet," Philia admitted with a wry grin.

"Just follow the old man's lead," He shrugged with a laugh while pulling off his shoes.

Chapter XLII - *Vervain*

Vervain is a popular remedy due to its multiple plant-beneficial compounds. Some of its benefits include antitumor effects, nerve cell protection, anxiety- and convulsion-reducing properties, and antimicrobial activity.

In Spiritual Work: *Vervain has both purification ability and protective properties. It is used for cleansing and consecrating a sacred ritual space. It is also a protective herb. For example, Roman soldiers would carry vervain into battle, and people would sprinkle their homes with vervain to keep away evil Spirits.*

Fortunately, the restaurant wasn't so busy on Monday morning that they needed a reservation. But Philia was happy she made one, so they didn't have to wait. The hostess sat them by the windows that overlooked the ocean. Philia was surprised to see a table from the restaurant outside in the sand for people to use. Jean was happily surprised, too. He was halfway out the door when Philia and Shaka looked up from the window and saw him, shoes in hand.

"Wait!" Philia called out,

Shaka just shook his head in exasperation,

"You'd better tell the hostess we're moving outside," he advised, getting off the table to follow his eccentric friend.

"These suede shoes are not meant for this," Philia replied, throwing her hands in the air,

"Why?" Asked Shaka, stopping to look at her feet with a raised eyebrow.

Philia felt like she had been yanked out of bed when she awoke with a start after an hour of lucid dreaming. She felt energized and alert, as though she had slept all night. Her mind buzzed while it compartmentalized all the information she'd been given. The first thing she did was get dressed before calling Leatrice. She wasn't certain of much. But she knew that many things. Still, she knew whatever Leatrice had found out could not be entrusted to her uncle. Now, she no longer felt guilty about keeping information from a man who had sold his heredity for wealth.

She had been speaking to Leatrice as quietly as possible when a knock forced her to cut the call short. Philia was now quietly listening and waiting to see who was outside.

After a moment, the knock came again.

"Hey, it's one o'clock. Are you getting ready yet?" Shaka asked softly on the other side of the door.

Before Shaka knew what was happening, Philia grabbed him by his perfectly pressed white-collared, short-sleeve polo shirt and yanked him into the room, closing the door and locking it behind him.

"Whoa, I'm trying to make a good first impression, young lady," Shaka confessed, straightening his shirt.

When he finally looked up, he found Philia was already dressed in a beautiful off-white, ankle-length dress and white strappy sandals. Her hair was in its usual bun, moving to and fro as she quietly paced the floor before him.

"Do you need help with something?" Shaka asked after a short while of watching Philia stare down at her feet.

"Shaka, how long have we known each other?"

"Over four years now," His face showed concern, "Why?"

"And I hope in all that time, I've proven to you that although I'm young, I'm not a person to give in to rash decisions or actions."

"Yeah, what's this about, Phil?"

Without a word, Philia reached up to put her right hand around the big man's neck. Shaka backed away reflexively.

"Trust me," She pleaded as she looked into his eyes and took a deep breath.

Philia had no idea what she was doing. Yet a voice told her she might be able to make the same Alta Major connection her aunt had made. To show Shaka something hidden in his past. She was not sure, but she hoped she was right.

"Trust me," She whispered again. Then, reaching up, Philia placed her hand on the base of Shaka's skull.

Her eyes gained a glow to them while her face became tranquil, and her breathing slowed. Within seconds, Shaka fell to his blue jean-covered knees, his torso arched backward, and his mouth widened as if he was letting out something deep inside.

The moment Philia's hand touched the back of his skull, Shaka's numbing pressure just above the center of his eyes since he started working with Jean began to vibrate, then burst with a loud whoosh in his head. His spine curved like a bolt of electricity was running down his body for a moment. Philia kept her hand steady on his neck as his eyes started rushing behind his closed eyelids.

****

Shaka thought he had an out-of-body experience when he saw himself kneeling in front of Philia. Even though he was standing next to her watching the exchange. In his mind, he heard Philia's voice,

"I'm having this experience with you. I'm not sure how,"

"Can you hear me?" he asked, his mind astounded by what was happening.

He thought this must be a dream when no answer came from her.

Yet, in his heart, he knew it wasn't.

The scene changed. Shaka found himself in South Africa, in his university classroom.

I looked good, he thought, admiring himself in fitted blue jeans, a white collared shirt, and a brown suit jacket.

He was giving a lecture on the religions of the sacred feminine. The Catholic and Christian patriarchal religions had depleted almost all-female-focused worshipping through their many wars. Shaka smiled, reliving that day. It was the day he'd met Jean.

Right then, the young lecturer spotted the old, pale white face in the sharp, dark suit sitting on one of the wooden chairs—a distinctive singularity. In the back of the half-moon-shaped room, full of young, brown faces listening to him intently.

He looks out of place. So, he thought then and now.

After the class ended, everyone left the room to let the next course in. Shaka watched as the old white guest joined the throng of excited students. He wondered then, as he was wondering now,

Why did the white man stay the whole lecture but never speak?

The scene changed again. The young Shaka was outside, just finishing signing copies of his book for some student fans. When he saw Jean, he walked through a hall with both sides lined with yellow-and-red, flower-filled shrubs towards his car. The old man was standing obscurely in a corner, having a conversation. The young man let his curiosity get the best of him and slowed to listen.

"Yes, I'm here. I have the page from The Book of the Ashanti to test his blood. And after this, you will tell me how to free my wife? I don't understand what that means. That wasn't part of the deal. You said you would give me what I need if I brought him to you. My wife's Spirit is stuck in that Book. You never told me that would happen. You said it would drain her, filling me

with enough continuous energy to read it. I can't live knowing her soul is trapped! Please, that is the only reason I'm doing this."

Jean begged into the phone as his voice cracked. His face was twisted, and he was on the verge of tears, a sheet of paper clenched in his other hand. The pain in the old man's voice was too familiar to the young man.

"Wait," Shaka spoke softly to no one, reliving what was now to him a crucial piece of forgotten history.

His mind was spinning as to what all of this might mean. Did Jean have The Book that belonged to his tribe this whole time?

Shaka's view changed again, but before anything could solidify, a knock on the door forced Philia to break the connection, leaving him woozily on his calves.

Philia took several deep breaths before answering,

"Yes, uncle?"

"*Cherie*, we have to go. Have you seen Shaka?"

"He's in here with me," Philia replied as the big man slowly returned to his feet. "We'll be right down."

"Wonderful. I'll see you guys downstairs," he replied in his usual cheerful manner.

Shaka looked visibly shaken, standing in front of Philia.

"Breathe," Philia directed, placing her palm on his chest and looking calmly into his eyes. Shaka followed her instruction, inhaling deeply, exhaling slowly, and feeling the vibration in his body dial down to a hum.

"The day after I accepted his offer," He started pacing slowly, "to come to work with him in America, he had a nurse come to my class to take blood from me. Jean said it was for medical clearance, for immigration," he spoke softly, but there was an underlying tone of anger or hurt, Philia thought.

"Part of that was true," Philia confirmed.

"I don't understand,"

"The immigration part, but I don't have time to explain now. I'm still attempting to understand it all myself. So please be patient with me," Philia pleaded as she opened the door to her room.

"How did you do that, that vision thing?" he whispered to her as they moved down the hall.

"I don't know. I didn't think I could. I'm not even sure how or why that vision came up, but I know it has to do with an energetic connection to The Divine," She told him while shaking her head in disbelief.

"Located at the base of the skull, it's called the Alta Major," She replied as she walked into the elevator.

"Alta Major," Shaka repeated thoughtfully, following her.

Philia tapped the back of her neck with one hand as she pushed the down button with the other. The large man placed his hand on the back of his neck, feeling a warm area at the base of his skull.

"The heat will dissipate quickly," she replied, not even looking back at him as the lift reached the first floor.

"Connection to the divine," Shaka mumbled softly as he followed her off the elevator, still touching the back of his neck, feeling the heat leaving.

Outside, Jean was smiling beside the Bel-Air, wearing another all-white linen outfit and a white fedora with a black band.

"How many linen outfits do you have, old man?" Shaka called out to him,

Philia could tell by the tone of his voice that he was struggling to maintain his optimistic composure. Shaka gave one of his dazzling smiles, but she could tell it was forced. Jean didn't notice that his friend and confident mind was about to explode. As Shaka tried to figure out if he had been manipulated and exploited all this time? Has it all been a ruse? Has Jean ever really been his friend?

"A lot," Philia answered for him, patting Shaka on the back as he opened the door for her and walked around to the driver's side,

"I think there was one summer where that was all my uncle wore," She tried to chuckle, but it came out dry.

"Is everything okay?" He asked, looking at her as he got in the front seat.

"*Oui*, of course, everything is great," She replied, knowing she was trying too hard. "Shaka was just helping with a stuck zipper," She finished, noticing that he already had a bouquet of white lilies in the seat next to her.

"Oh, okay." Jean seemed satisfied with the answer.

"Don't worry, old man. We're not plotting against you," Shaka answered pointedly, looking Jean directly in the eyes with a smile that, if Jean had known better, would have caused him to feel more fear than his chuckle indicated.

"I guess not," Jean chuckled, closing the car door.

Luckily, the drive to the house where they met Leatrice for lunch was only ten minutes from Jean's home on the island. This surprised everyone in the car as they turned onto the street that the GPS on Philia's phone indicated. Suddenly, Jean had a case of déjà vu. It passed quickly, but Jean felt he had once taken a ride down this street with his family on a Sunday morning, perhaps even in this car.

The car pulled into the circular driveway lined with exotic flowers and plants, and Shaka parked behind a black Jeep Wrangler. It was much smaller than Jean's home. Yet, all the passengers felt specific magnetic energy emanating from it. The house had a detectable presence to it, Jean observed. Like the kind of house he once visited with the twins. Nevertheless, in the front seat, he acted like he was going on a date. Jean straightened his clothes, smoothing out the front of his shirt, and checked his teeth to ensure nothing was stuck between them.

Satisfied, he asked Philia for the bouquet of white lilies he'd placed in the seat next to her while coming out of the car to let his niece out. However, Philia had already slid to the other side and was being escorted out of the vehicle by Shaka. Jean frowned as he turned around only to see Leatrice descending the front steps, causing all ill feelings of slightness to instantly disappear.

She was wearing a fitted, yellow sweater dress with a V-neck and a hemline that landed mid-thigh. Her hair was loose, framing her face like a halo. While the sun moving westward behind her made her glow. Neither Jean nor Shaka noticed they were openly gawking at

Leatrice. Until Philia cleared her throat as she walked past them to greet the doctor.

"You look amazing," Philia advised, "To think you've been hiding all of this under a lab coat." Then, she teased, kissing her on both cheeks before whispering, "When can we talk?"

"Soon," Leatrice whispered with a smile.

Jean came walking up, finally regaining his composure.

"Amazing," He whistled, "This is not coming from your boss, just a man who thinks you look fantastic, and these are for our host," He offered, handing Leatrice the bouquet.

"But now I feel like I should have brought more flowers."

"Yes, you should have. Just have the whole shop delivered; you can afford it," Shaka quipped as he joined the group. "I must say you are breathtaking," he admitted, bending down to kiss Leatrice on the cheek.

"Thanks for the compliments. I might have to steal some of Ceres' clothes after all this," She laughed.

"Come, let me introduce you to our host for the afternoon."

Inside the house, three women stood in the living room, waiting to receive their guests. Now, back to herself, Maggie was the first to meet them.

"Oh, my goodness, it's you!" Jean exclaimed, rushing past everyone to greet her.

"Yup, and now we get to thank you properly," she smiled, taking hold of both of his hands.

Shaka had almost forgotten everything he had been thinking about when his eyes landed on Diana in the blue dress. If a man of his complexion could blush, Shaka was afraid he would have resembled a tomato. But, instead, he was frozen in the entryway, unable to move. Until Ceres walked up to the big man, kissed him on the cheek, and then escorted him with a smile into the living room where everyone else was gathering.

"Thank you for my birthday," Ceres acknowledged both men. "We had to rush out that night, so we didn't have time to properly thank you,"

"Yes," Diana admitted, bringing up the rear. "Thank you. We're not normally so taken aback by someone's generosity that we run away rather than face them."

She looked at each new member warmly and kissed them on the cheek, saving Shaka for last.

"It was our pleasure," Jean replied, almost giddy, looking over at Shaka, who was trying hard not to keep looking at Diana.

"Yeah," Jean continued with a smirk, stepping over to elbow Shaka in the side.

"It was our pleasure," he repeated,

"Yes, our pleasure," Shaka concurred, finally finding his voice. Then, causing everyone to laugh, Diana took Shaka's arm to lead him to the couch.

"My mother is upstairs," Leatrice informed everyone as they sat. "She'll be down in a moment,"

"Bonjour," Gerda called to everyone below as she started down the stairs in a satin yellow ankle-length A-line dress with spaghetti straps.

Jean turned to look up the stairs and shot to his feet as if the floor had burned him. Shaka and Philia turned too — and went equally still.

"Everyone, this is my mother, Gerda," Leatrice announced cheerfully to the guests, but her smile faded when she saw the look on their faces.

"How are you, beautiful people doing today?" Gerda continued, descending the stairs slowly. Jean moved to her side faster than anyone expected to escort her down the remaining few stairs.

"Madam, you look...." Jean trailed off.

"You look beautiful," He finished, his eyes welling with tears.

"What's wrong?" she asked, worried, putting an arm around him and leading him back to the couch.

"You look almost identical to my late aunt," Philia replied to her softly. "Different hair color and eyes, but everything else...you guys could be sisters."

"I've only seen a picture," Shaka advised, "but the resemblance is undeniable,"

Jean kissed her cheek in greeting.

"I apologize. I am not a man who easily gives in to emotions. But seeing you...." He looked at her and choked up.

"I understand," Gerda said. "I lost my husband, too. But I would probably be much more emotional than you now if I saw someone walking toward me who looked like him. He was the love of my life," She felt a tightening in her throat as the words came out.

For a moment, the room was silent. Then, finally, Maggie got up.

"Well, this isn't the day for sad tears. We have a room full of wonderful new people to entertain. And we've been working on my mother's famous sangria all morning. So, I'm going to start pouring drinks and telling funny stories. Shaka, you come with me. I need big hands," She demanded as she walked away into the kitchen with Shaka following close behind.

Chapter XLIII – *Milk Thistle*

Milk thistle contains compounds that may support skin, liver, and bone health and enhance weight loss. Milk thistle might also help prevent insulin resistance and slow cancer growth, among other benefits.

In Spiritual Work: *Carry this herb with you or leave it in a bowl. It will renew vitality. It is used as a protective amulet in mojo bags alongside other anti-hexing and cleansing herbs.*

Leatrice and Gerda took a seat as Ceres questioned her sister,

"Well, yes. Like last night when I invoked Ayizan's name. And by the way, I have no idea where that came from. I think she was expecting another Priestess. Ayizan isn't saying 'SEER. Ayizan is saying, 'SEE HER.' I've heard it over and over. Since late Saturday, I didn't understand where it came from or what it meant until now. So, maybe your presence, Cee, made our connection stronger."

"So why is she only speaking to you?"

"I don't know. I think what you were going through, the sudden unbalance of energy, may have awakened Ayizan. When she showed up and didn't find her Priestess. I was the closest person here to a Reader she could find, and she's stuck on me until we find her Priestess. Maybe she's not strong enough, or her Priestess is lost? I just don't know?" Magalie tried to explain but was as uncertain as the women around her.

'What I don't understand," Leatrice started thoughtfully, her heartbeat returning to a modicum of normalcy,

"Is why now? I mean, Cee has been home with you all day. You say you have been hearing her voice for two days. So why did she appear now and not earlier?"

"I think I may have a clue as to what's going on," Diana called out as she entered the room and placed her bag on the living room table.

The women turned in surprise. No one had heard her come in. Diana was the only person who could walk in and out of the house without the alarm sounding.

"Jean Dieudonne was one of the men that paid for our dinner last night,"

Leatrice felt the air leave her.

"What are you talking about?" Ceres asked, moving from the kitchen to the living room where Diana stood.

Diana pulled Shaka's book out of her purse and handed it to her daughter with the author's photo visible. Ceres was surprised to see the man, who was smitten with her mother, on the back cover. Yet, even more, she was astonished at the vèvè design in the front.

"Do you recognize him or that?" Diana questioned Ceres and Leatrice

Leatrice looked over at the book and answered before Ceres.

"That's Shaka Solomon. He's a historian at ARTS Tower. Also, he is a partner of Jean Dieudonne, but I don't understand what he would have to do with this. I've heard they met after Mrs. Dieudonne passed. Jean was out of sorts and went to South Africa for healing. He met Shaka at the University of South Africa, and has worked together ever since. After I made his acquaintance on Friday, I asked some faculty friends about him. Everyone seemed to agree he was a nice guy, but the thing is, no one knew anything about him, nothing solid. Just a lot of exaggerated rumors running around."

"Like what?" questioned Ceres.

"Well," Leatrice attempted to recount some of the information, rubbing at her eye underneath the glasses. "He's the first son of a tribal Chieftain, heir to a throne. He has three wives, but none he loves, and he's over here looking for his true love." Diana rolled her eyes at that part. "Oh, and he has magical powers, which now I'm beginning to think might be true."

"Oh," Ceres answered, turning to Leatrice while handing Shaka's book to Magalie for her to look at the picture.

"When did I happen?" Leatrice paused. "I came down Saturday, right after stealing the page. Do you think they follow me?"

"First, you didn't steal it," Gerda commented from the couch, sucking her teeth, "and second, I doubt that. They were at the restaurant while you were with me," Gerda finished, motioning her daughter to join her on the couch so she could put an arm around her. "It's just a coincidence," Gerda tried to reassure Leatrice, hugging her tightly.

"There's no such thing as coincidences," the three Bastille women answered simultaneously. Causing Leatrice to groan in her mother's arms.

"I know," The young doctor replied softly.

"Something brought them into our path," Diana commented to no one in particular, "Do you recognize the vèvè?" She asked Ceres.

"I'm not sure," Ceres shrugged, unable to place the lightning bolt with the two arrows crossing over it. Although Ceres was focused on it, her mind was still occupied by Ayizan's visit.

"I know dark forces are looking for The Books, too. I kinda saw or maybe felt. I don't know exactly. It was vague, but I'm sure I saw two men in that vision last night on the beach with Ceres," Magalie confessed.

"What?" Her mom and sister shouted.

"Okay, Mags, what the fuck else are you not telling us?" Ceres snapped.

"No less than you!" Magalie countered.

"You saw them in a vision, knowing I didn't, and you didn't tell anyone?"

"I couldn't be sure you hadn't seen them, and I didn't know what it meant. I'm still not sure it's the same two men. I didn't see faces, just a feeling it was two men, old and powerful." she finished reflectively.

"Everyone, breathe," Diana interrupted as their guests looked on mutely.

"There's too much going on for this. Right now is not the time for you guys to fight each other. There are many more things to focus on, and I need you guys to help."

Magalie looked at Shaka's book in her hand and then at her family's Book. She smiled. "Maybe he's the connection we need for Ayizan. That's the next step to learn what's going on." She looked at her mother, then asked, "Ceres, what're the plans for the wine you told us about?"

"No," Diana answered, plain and simple.

"But, mam," Ceres pleaded, "you haven't even heard anything yet. I know what I'm doing now. It'll be perfect."

"The last time I found out about your plans with wine, I had to take the kid cookies spiked with ginger and dandelion root to calm his fears of the *madichon* you put in his head," Diana replied.

"Mother," Ceres giggled at John, thinking he was cursed with bad luck because he was cheating on women and in school.

"That guy deserved to fail his classes! Plus, everything worked out in the end. He retook the semester, passed his classes honestly, and stayed clear of Dax and me. That's all I wanted out of it,"

"Mom, it's the simplest and fastest way to get the information we need," Magalie added.

"No," Diana repeated, already feeling the loss of a battle not yet fought.

Taking a deep breath, Magalie looked up at her mother. Her hazel eyes were clear and focused. "It's the fastest and safest way, Mom. We need to know things."

"Ugh, of course, the Seer is probably right," Diana admitted, emphasizing the last part through a clenched jaw. She put her hand on Magalie's shoulder. "Never before has there been a Seer and Priestess in the same family. Never have I seen so much synchronicity."

"She's not a Seer," Ceres answered off the cuff, returning to the items in the kitchen. "Apparently, Ayizan has hijacked Mags until we find her Priestess,"

"Wait, what?" Diana turned around to face Ceres in the kitchen.

"Exactly," Ceres continued, "She was just here," she shrugged, "didn't speak to anyone except Mags. She hasn't been saying SEER. She's been asking us to *see her*."

"Oh, thank God," Diana breathed, hugging Magalie tightly, "A Seer and a Priestess, that's just too much for me to handle right now."

Magalie frowned,

"You don't think I can handle it?" Magalie questioned her mom as she wiggled her way out of the embrace,

"That is not what I'm saying, and you know it!" Diana advised, holding her hands, "You two can handle anything. It's me I'm worried about.

I'm not as strong as I used to be. I wouldn't even know how to help a Seer right now,"

"Anyways," Ceres interjected, "We were trying to figure out why she decided to materialize now. Mags says she has been hearing her since Saturday night, and apparently, she was the one who helped Mags get me under control last night,"

"Saturday, I came down with the page from Jean's Book," Leatrice shouted, "It has been nearby the whole time. I only just brought it inside,"

The doctor popped out of her seat, walking towards the folder as her mind started to piece things together.

"Maybe this is the connection to her?" Leatrice asked excitedly, handing Diana the page.

"Some confusion with her Reader dead, her Book lost, and a page of it being here right when you came into your power," Diana rambled while holding onto the page.

"She took me as the next best thing?" But, Magalie questioned, her face askew, "If her Reader is dead, shouldn't The Book have found a new line of guardians? Isn't that how it works to keep the flow of knowledge uninterrupted?"

"That is how it's supposed to work. Unless another Reader in the family is strong enough to hold the line there, another firstborn daughter," Diana affirmed.

"Reader?" Leatrice asked, confused.

"It's another name for a Priestess," Gerda answered her daughter. "She, who can read and use The Book to its fullest potential."

"Besides Jean's wife, he had no other Reader?" Magalie questioned.

"Oh. I know Jean only has one son. And his son's been out of the picture for a while now, on missionary trips. Why do you ask?"

"Do you know anything about his wife's family? Did his wife have any sisters?" Magalie continued

"There's not a lot of information out there about his wife. She was a very private person, from what I've heard. A lot of her philanthropy was done anonymously late in her life. It was only revealed by people after her death as a tribute."

Magalie looked up toward Ceres. "Her, the Teacher, wants me to discover what might be with Jean. I'm sure of it."

"Maybe it's someone down here, a grandchild. How old is his son?" Gerda questioned.

"Nope," Leatrice chimed in. "From what I know, Mateo Dieudonne is very single. Jean has no grandkids."

"Money can buy a lot of silence," Diana said quietly.

"Very true."

"Spiked wine it is, then," Ceres confirmed with a laugh.

"We'll call that plan B for now," Maggie said. "Something better might come up. It's only ten a.m."

Diana laughed weakly; too much had happened so fast, and she was still weak. She had not slept last night with everything that had happened. Today, she felt like she was unlikely to get any rest. The family's matriarch needed to regroup her energy, not to mention to rest her back.

"Diana, why don't you get some sleep? Leatrice and I need to go home and freshen up. Say we meet back at twelve to go grocery shopping?" Gerda suggested as if reading her friend's mind.

"Sounds perfect," Diana agreed, silently thanking the gods. "But before you leave Leatrice, you should call Jean. We need to figure out what his connection is to all this." Diana finished as she retrieved Leatrice's phone from inside her bag and handed it to her.

Leatrice took the phone as she sat down next to her mother. She looked at all the women around her for reassurance. Then, taking a deep breath, Leatrice pushed the callback button on her phone.

Chapter XLIV - *Ginseng*

Commonly touted for its antioxidant and anti-inflammatory effects. It could also help regulate blood sugar levels and benefit certain types of cancer. Ginseng also strengthens the immune system, enhances brain function, reduces fatigue, and improves symptoms of erectile dysfunction.

In Spiritual Work: *Ginseng is a "Wonder of the World Root" that will grant a wish etched onto a root placed under running water. To make a Success Satchel, place Ginseng Root, Black Cohosh, Red Clover, and John the Conqueror Root with Iron Pyrite in a bag.*

The women had changed into dry clothing and sat in the living room, discussing what had happened. Ceres sat on the arm of the couch, resting her head on her sister's shoulder, wrapped tightly in her Batman throw blanket. The young Priestess felt a deep calm now that she was one with Spirit — and a quiet grief, because she understood the full scope of what she was and what she would be asked to carry. Not just for herself, but for the millions who had spent their lives under persecution.

"I'm not sure how to explain it," Ceres lifted herself to speak, "It's like, yes, there is chaos, but there is an order to it; we are the directive. So, when God created life, he took chaos, the free energy that flows through all things, and gave it direction in life."

"Okay, I follow," Leatrice affirmed, leaning in from her position on the loveseat next to Magalie.

Ceres was working through the genealogy between Adam, Eve, and Lilith — as far as she understood it — and how all of them fit into the picture.

"When the first Man and Woman were created, that order was given reason. Unlike the other creations, we could learn and direct the chaos we're made from because we have free will. We didn't have to follow the laws of nature it had created for other animals. But we still have to follow the Universal Laws." Ceres paused, tapping The Book on the coffee table before her.

"Lilith and Adam were in balance. When he tried to dominate her, she used her free will to free herself from bondage, but the Creator kept the balance with their children. Over time, as more of Lilith's descendants fell under domination, the balance and our ability to use free will degraded."

"Yeah, all we have to do is look at what women are facing today, yesterday, and tomorrow to see how the balance is screwed," Leatrice commented.

The women nodded in agreement with her comment,

"What I don't understand is if the one cardinal rule of balance has been thrown out the window, why doesn't The Creator step in and fix it?" Diana asked, leaning across the table.

"The deal," Magalie said quietly, rolling her shoulders.

"Exactly," Ceres confirmed, "it breaks down like this," Ceres started loosening the blanket from around her, "when Lilith ran away from the garden, and although she was coerced into making that deal. She used her free will, and The Creator, as wise and omnipotent as They are, cannot interfere with deals we make using our free will. So, we must ride out all of this shit until it is time for the meek to inherit the Earth. It is supposed to happen when the Earth tilts on its axis again. Then, Four blood moons rise into the sky. Afterward, the children of Lilith will be free to learn how to release themselves from those that seek to dominate."

Taking a deep breath, Ceres sat back and looked at her mother,

"I don't know the exact date of the event that will start the shift. I know that Lilith's descendants were scattered during the slave trade. There are other Books, other Priestesses. And so far, The Books have stood apart to prevent the secret knowledge within. The knowledge Lilith gave them was stifled by those seeking to destroy The Books and keep Lilith's descendants in bondage. Only when they are connected will we learn the full scope of Lilith's teachings and be truly free." Then Ceres looked at Gerda.

"All of us in this room are directly connected to The Books. When the time comes, all our strength will be needed,"

Leatrice picked up The Book, thinking about Ceres' words. Did it make sense that she had the bloodline because she was Haitian, or was there something else? So much had happened in such a short time. Leatrice forgot about why she had initially come here to speak to Diana.

"I'll get the wine," Magalie said. She patted Leatrice on the back, leaving her staring at The Book, deep in thought.

Gerda watched her daughter; her heart was heavy. Years ago, her late husband and Diana realized they were first cousins. Diana had confided in Gerda and asked her to watch for any changes in Leatrice when she turned twenty-two. After that birthday, Gerda had observed her daughter slowly shed Christianity for the Orishas, but nothing else happened. Now, Gerda wondered if her decision had been the best.

Magalie returned from the kitchen juggling three wine bottles and plastic cups when her sister saw her and ran to help, her steps light as a feather.

"You know, there are only five of us," Ceres jokes, taking hold of two bottles.

"I know. I couldn't carry anymore, or I would've." Magalie retorted, lowering her voice. She wondered, "So, you are going to not tell Mom everything, like the dark shadows we saw us facing before the tides pulled us out of those shared visions,"

"I don't know. How much did you see?" Ceres asked, stopping to look at her sister.

"Not enough, I guess. All it would do is scare everyone right now."

"Exactly,"

"So, will you tell me how you did that light beam thing?" Magalie winked.

"As soon as I figure it out," Ceres laughed.

Chapter XLV – *Bay Leaf*

Bay leaf is a good source of vitamin A, vitamin B6, and vitamin C. These vitamins are all known to support a healthy immune system. Bay leaf tea can help ease bouts of upset stomachs. It can help relieve sinus pressure or a stuffy nose. Reduces type 2 diabetes risk factors.

In Spiritual Work: *Use the leaves to write down things you wish to manifest or release and then burn them in ritual. Keep bay leaves on your person when performing any healing rituals or when you're about to do something that you want to succeed at.*

By the time Philia changed tables with the staff's help, the guys outside had already buried their feet in the sand at a different table. Philia sighed as she told the team, never mind. She sat beside Shaka, watching Jean on the phone further down the beach.

"Leatrice finally called him back," he answered before she even had a chance to pose the question. "He's been trying to get in touch with her since God knows when this morning,"

Down the beach, Jean was thrilled Leatrice had called him back and even happier to hear she was close by.

"You're in Fort Pierce! Us," they heard the old man say into the phone as he started walking back towards them.

"Well, me, Shaka, and Philia. *Oui, Oui*, she is here, too. I am sure the office will fall into ruins without her there." Jean laughed and winked in Philia's direction. "You should join us for breakfast. We are just sitting down. Philia, what is the name of this place?"

"Sharky's Beach Café."

"Sharky's Beach Café," he repeated into the phone. "They are letting us eat outside. I have my feet in the sand." He chuckled, apparently amused with himself. "Well, come with all of them, Shaka's treat,"

Shaka groaned as Jean sat beside him and teasingly used his elbow to nudge the big man. On the other side of the phone, Diana advised Leatrice what to say. The ladies had decided that since all roads seemed to lead to Jean. It would be better to face things head-on by inviting Jean and Shaka for lunch at the Bastille house.

"No, I understand. But, yes, let's plan for lunch. Yes, two should be fine, and we'll discuss your latest findings then. But, no, Leatrice, you need to relax. It is all puzzling to us, too. The answers will come. Remember the old hermetic saying–the teacher will appear when the student is ready. Okay, talk to you soon. *Adieu.*" Jean hung up the phone.

"What did she say?" Shaka asked immediately.

"She is down here, apparently, to speak to a friend of her mother's, an expert in old languages. Leatrice hoped that Diana could date a symbol she saw on the page. She will tell us more about it when we meet for lunch, but besides that, she has more questions than answers."

"I love that you're making plans for lunch when you haven't even eaten breakfast," Shaka chuckled, amused, "Did she tell you anything about the symbol?"

Jean chuckled. "One must always know where their next meal is coming from,"

"What page?" Philia questioned, at a loss as to what was going on. Shaka and Jean exchanged looks before Jean replied to her.

"I had a page from your aunt's Book. I was trying to date it to get some more information from it. It's the only thing I have left since The Book went missing,"

"Oh," Philia replied quietly. "I didn't know that's what you were using her for. She's not the expert we usually use to date antique paper."

"I know, but she had other qualifications that I thought were just as important. So, I didn't want to bother you with the details," Jean smiled, reaching over to squeeze her hand.

"As for what symbol, my guess is as good as yours, Shaka. I thought everything was faded except the lines she told us about."

"Faded?" Philia questioned, the sense of uneasiness returning.

She felt sick about not telling Jean about Mateo's call or The Book. He seemed so genuinely worried about where it was.

"Yeah, The Book's words started to fade before your aunt passed," not a complete lie, Jean reasoned, "Were you able to read it since," He paused, thinking, "Actually, can you remember the last time you saw The Book?"

"A few months before *Tante* died, I think," she lied.

"Huh, I see," Jean let go of her hand, rubbing his chin thoughtfully, "Did you get a chance to see Mateo the day before he left?"

"No." She replied a little too quickly. "I mean, we tried to see each other, but it just ended up on a video call instead,"

"Oh, well, at least you got that," He sighed, "I think I got an email two weeks ago letting me know he was turning off his GPS, but no information on the reasons why."

"Are you expecting him anytime soon?" Shaka asked as the waitress came out with a water pitcher and glasses.

"Something tells me soon,"

"I hope so," Philia confessed with a smile, hoping she was hiding her heart pounding in her chest from anxiety.

I was not built to keep secrets, Philia realized.

"I'm starving," Jean added to no one in particular.

"Aren't you always?" Shaka chuckled jokingly as the waitress returned to their table with food.

"Excuse me." Shaka started to lift his hand to stop the waitress, thinking she had the wrong table, but Philia guided his hand back down.

"I placed an order with our reservation," she informed them, still smiling, "We don't want him to start claiming we are starving him to death." She pointed to her uncle, who already had a piece of crepe in his mouth. "Even if it wasn't our food, it's too late now."

Shaka shook his head, directing the waitress to finish putting the food before him.

"Lobster crepe, nice," he winked, pleased with Philia's choice since that was precisely what he would order.

"Was it a good guess?" the young woman asked her senior.

"It's like you read my mind,"

"I wish. I'm just really good at guessing what people around me need,"

"And providing it to them; a family trait, from what I have come to experience,"

"Yeah," she replied softly, her attention split.

Philia's eyes had been drawn to a group of young adults by the water. They looked to be in their twenties, like her. From their light pale complexion, Philia assumed they must be vacationing from the north. She kind of envied them. Here she was, a young woman in her twenties who lived in the land of vacations, but this was probably her first time by the water all year. There were three guys in the group and three girls. She wondered if they were all paired up. Did they go to the movies? Have wild, drug-filled parties? Smoke weed? All the things she had never done in her life.

Philia sighed as she watched one of the girls wearing a tiny bikini run up and jump into one of the guy's welcoming arms. He stumbled backward a few steps before recovering his stance. They laughed at the miss, tumbled into the water, and kissed passionately. Their outlines were highlighted by the morning sun.

This could have been a postcard, Philia thought.

A flash of light from the girl's hand drew Philia's attention.

With Beyonce's song in mind, she thought he amusingly put a ring on it. Before coming to America from France, Philia's mother told her to experience as much life as possible.

Sighing, she returned to her food, picking at things without eating. Philia was picking up her glass of water when she suddenly felt someone was watching. That feeling is when you're standing somewhere, and someone is staring at you from across the room. She put the glass down to look around, scanning the restaurant. Then, blocking the sun with her hand, she looked around the beach for anyone familiar. The second time around, she locked eyes with this handsome blonde in floral shorts and great abs. He was standing among the group but alone, staring at her unabashedly. She quickly put her head down as soon as he caught her eyes. Her cheeks flushed pink enough for Shaka to take notice. The older man looked down at her, turned, and looked behind him.

"Ah." Shaka winked at her, seeing what was happening. Philia groaned.

"What?" Jean asked, finally slowing down on his gluttonous eating.

"Nothing," Philia replied quickly. Pleading Shaka with her eyes to leave it be, she turned to her uncle, changing the subject, "So, why are you guys down here?"

"Honestly, I don't know." Jean reached across to take food from Philia's plate. "So far, I think we may have found Shaka, a wife," he grinned.

"Wait, what?"

"Nothing," Shaka quickly replied, shaking his head, "Your uncle is nothing but trouble. He is lucky he found the love of his life when she was young. He doesn't know anything about how to properly court a woman. He moves too fast,"

"Absurd," Jean replied. "It was a birthday, and you bought them dinner,"

"I didn't even know her name. Now she thinks I'm a show-off."

"Do you think that is true, Philia?" the older man asked, wanting a female's insight.

"I guess it all depends on the woman. Plus, I can't speak on the subject since I wasn't there," She offered contemptuously.

"Je suis désolé, please forgive me for the late invite," Her uncle turned to her with a puppy face, "I'll make it up to you. Still, I'm pretty sure

I'm right about this." Jean continued. "We will run into the future, Mrs. Solomon, again."

Shaka groaned.

"May the Gods lead us," Philia replied with a chuckle,

Outside the restaurant and getting back in the car, Philia wondered what she would do if she found The Book. It was one thing to lie about the last time she'd seen it. But to lie to him once she had it when her uncle seemed to want to find it so severely felt wrong. Especially since she wasn't sure why she should. Mateo's message was cryptic, leaving her to wonder if her uncle was part of some secret organization, which he clearly could not have been. She had grown close to the old man in the last few years. The pain he felt for losing his wife was real, and so were his efforts to try and mend the space between him and Mateo.

"You, okay?" Jean asked her, catching her far-off in thought.

"Yeah, I'm fine. I'm just thinking about Mateo. I hope he's okay, wherever he is," she said, reaching for the rosary under her white blouse.

"I'm sure he is," Her uncle replied reassuringly.

The drive back to the house in Bethel Creek was as uneventful as their ride to the restaurant. As they pulled into the circular driveway, Philia felt like she always did, like a child coming to this place. The big house on the beach with its white stone wall reminded her of a fairy tale. She always imagined she was Ariel, forcing her cousin to be Sebastian as they hid from King Triton, better known as Tonton Jean. It had been a magical time for her here, even when Esperanza became too sick to accompany them to the beach.

That morning, when Philia stepped out of the car, she had to admit, the house didn't feel the same. She stepped back to look at it and paused. A woman in white was looking down at her through the window of the library on the second floor.

"U*ncle*," she called out to Jean, about to ask if he had someone in the house,

"Yes?"

But when Philia looked up again, the woman was nowhere to be found. The movement of a Royal Palm fawn's reflection on the glass from the front lawn caught her eye. Maybe she had been mistaken.

"Nothing," she replied, walking up to the front doors with Shaka.

Philia moved from the solid glass wall to the deep, comfortable living room couches, roaming around the vast, remarkable house like it was her first time there in years. Everything was the same as the last time she'd stepped inside. Eventually, she joined the men in the kitchen to ensure they entertained themselves enough and no one would miss her when she went hunting.

Jean had just come up from the cellar with a few bottles of wine. And placed them on the granite island counter they were sitting at. Philia could see by the labels only one of the bottles was meant for drinking. This indicated to Philia that Shaka was about to get a free, even if unwanted, education in rare wines.

"This, my friend, is a Domaine de la Romanée-Conti Romance Grand Cru, 1972," Jean advised, "we paid a little over ten thousand dollars for it at auction," smiling as he gently handed the bottle to a very hesitant Shaka.

"You paid," Philia corrected, shaking her head.

"You were there. I don't remember you stopping me," Jean chuckled.

"But why, I mean seriously, why?" Shaka asked, inspecting every inch of the bottle.

"Well, it's several things," Jean started, ever the trader of rare things and always ready to impart knowledge as to why things are worth what they are,

"The production, of course, the smaller the batches made, the rarer. The vintage, where is the wine from, the grapes' history,"

"I didn't know grapes had a history,"

"All things have a history, my friend, all things,"

"Ahhh," Philia yawned, "If you guys don't mind, I think I'll nap before lunch. I didn't get much sleep,"

"Of course, Cheri, we will be fine," Jean smiled.

"I'll be fine as long one of these bottles is getting opened soon," Shaka chuckled, winking at his friend.

Chapter XLVI - *Allspice*

Allspice refers to the dried berries of the plant *Pimenta dioica*. It was given that name because its flavor combines cinnamon, nutmeg, cloves, pepper, juniper, and ginger. It has anti-inflammatory properties, aids digestion, boosts immunity, contains antioxidants, helps with dental health, and improves circulation.

In Spiritual Work: *Allspice is used in spells for money, luck, and healing. Burn-dried allspice for these functions or carry the berries in a satchel for the same purpose. In addition, Allspice is helpful in all healing mixtures.*

"Tell us the truth, great old liar.
Tell us the truth this day.
Young rabbits may play alone in the briar.
But we three were not born this May.
Oh, loosen your tongue, the great old liar.
Feel the freedom and release of the truth.
Throw your worries and cares into the fire.
And regain the light heart of your youth."

The three youngest women were in the kitchen, rhythmically repeating lines of text from The Book. They were breaking down herbs with their fingertips into a large glass pitcher. The pitcher already contained two bottles of red wine, cherries, apples, pineapple, the bluebell tincture, and the essence of licorice root.

"Remember to keep the vision of Jean's throat chakra opening to reveal the truth to us," Ceres would remind them often.

After Leatrice's conversation with Jean, their plans had changed somewhat; Diana still went upstairs to get some sleep. However, Gerda and Leatrice finally had a sit-down about her lineage before Gerda headed home with Leatrice staying behind to help the girls.

"The words are as important as the ingredients," Ceres explained to Leatrice. "But the words are for our *lwa*; their vibrations focus our energy and connect us to them."

"The universe is made of vibration. Our abilities are wrapped around using these vibrations to our advantage." Maggie picked up from where her sister had left off.

"Rhymes are a vibrational pattern we can create and use to focus our energy on whatever we are trying to manifest. That's why Indigenous people, African people, Hindus, Buddhists, and whoever else believes in the Spiritual plane of energy use vibrations when seeking help from their Spirit Guides. Whether with drums, dance, singing, or chanting, we pound the ground with our feet, and that vibration ripples across the universe," Magalie accented this thought by shooting her hand into the air like a rocket.

"That's why black churches can't be as docile and boring as white churches; there is no Spirit there for us. We are spoken to by the Spirits through the vibrations we cause, and that's also why great musicians are pretty much spellcasters." Magalie finished, winking at Leatrice, who was barely looking at them.

"In the beginning, there was the word," Leatrice quoted, her mind distracted.

"Exactly," Ceres confirmed.

Ceres looked over at her little sister for confirmation of her desire. Their mother had told them about Leatrice's lineage before she went to bed. The girls weren't exactly sure what Gerda had told her. However, Ceres and Magalie felt like

Leatrice needed to know everything. So, they decided to open a dialogue with her and fill in whatever missing pieces.

Magalie took a deep breath and nodded her head.

The ladies finished with the sangria, and Ceres relocated the pitcher, placing it on a flat clear disc of clear crystal quartz on the kitchen counter. The young Priestess stood before it with both palms facing down, repeating the rhyme thrice. Each time with more intensity than the last, the energy in the room felt electrified by the third repetition. She exhaled slowly as she spoke the last word, letting the power flow from her and over the elixir.

Only the sound of the crashing waves and the birds searching for their next meal outside disturbed the peace inside the house. The two women sitting at the kitchen counter watched the young Priestess work.

"We should talk," Ceres advised as she finished, turning to Leatrice with a knowing smile.

The young woman moved around to take the professor's hand, leading her to the beach as Magalie followed them. Ceres took a seat on the sand in front of the altar. Leatrice sat between her and Magalie, with the remnants of the fire between them and the ocean.

"So, Doc, Mom told me we're cousins," Magalie started, digging her toes into the warm seashore.

"Apparently," Leatrice answered, breathing deeply, "It's amazing when you find out that you are part of that, stupid Haitian men, misogynist bullshit, of having a second family,"

"I know it sucks. I've had friends who have found sisters they didn't know about on *Facebook*. And I know my mom was hurting. I mean, to find out you have a brother you didn't know about. And then, he dies while you're trying to save his life. And that was her only living relative besides us. It's a lot! I mean, shit, all of this, plus all of that, Fuckkkkk!" Ceres shouted, raising her hand to the sky.

Leatrice laughed, "Seriously, FUCK!"

The two women fell into each other, laughing until Leatrice had tears in her eyes.

Magalie shook her head, laughing at them as she pulled her vape pen out and took a hit.

"I'm glad to see all of that *edumacation* has increased your vocabularies, doctors," Scorned, shaking her head with a smirk,

"You know we love you, right? We're family. We've already been through some stuff together," Ceres leaned over to kiss Leatrice, and they started laughing anew.

"If only Mom could hear you now," Magalie jokes, "So, what else did the old ladies tell you?"

"Your ancestor." Leatrice stopped. "I mean, our ancestor," she corrected, clearing her throat, "is no other than Cécile Fatiman." She laughed derisively, causing Maggie to laugh too, which became her coughing. Leatrice reached over, patting her back as she released a smoke cloud.

"Heavy, right?"

"Right," Leatrice replied, taking hold of the vape pen.

"Hey, don't they drug test at the lab?" Ceres asked, surprised by her actions.

"We just put together a tonic that we're planning on drugging my boss with; I think me failing a drug test is the least of my worries at this point,"

Magalie and Ceres shook their head in agreement, chuckling.

"*Carpe Diem!*" Magalie exclaimed.

"*Carpe Diem.*"

"What else?" Ceres asked Leatrice.

Leatrice shrugged.

"I'm guessing it's because of this relationship between us that the page reacted when I bled on it."

"Exactly," confirmed Magalie.

"But the Priestess of that generation can use The Book's full power, whatever that means," Leatrice finished with a sigh.

"So far, I figured out I can speak to our direct line of ancestors when I need to," Ceres confirmed, "I'm guessing that's part of my Spirit being intertwined as one with them, but also a separate part of the whole since I'm still living. The Book responds by showing me what I'm looking for before I know what I need, but there's more."

"It's symbiotic, from what I've figured out," Leatrice concurred.

"I'm a vessel of some kind, I guess," Maggie shrugged.

"What were the ancestors thinking?" Ceres quipped.

"I don't think they had anything to do with this; this seems to be a wild card," Maggie replied.

"You're probably right."

"So, what does that mean?" Asked Leatrice, reaching for the vape pen again. "I know she told you things and helped Ceres last night."

"I honestly don't know." Magalie shrugged.

Leatrice started to snicker for no reason as she inhaled. "If not now, then when?" she shouted dramatically, laughing harder. Maggie looked at Ceres and shook her head.

"I think you've had enough, Doc," Maggie counsels, taking the vape pen from Leatrice.

"Yeah, you're probably right. I was never good with that stuff in school."

"Me neither," agreed Ceres.

"Another reason I'm the cool one is that you guys are too stuck in your head. You need to feel things to truly see,"

"Okay, whatever," Leatrice chuckled, "subsequently, anybody knows what's my part in all this?"

"Honestly, I don't," Ceres Shrugged

"That's easy. The power of three, duh," Maggie shouted.

"Stop," Ceres begged, rolling her eyes and making Leatrice chuckle.

"Seriously. It's all about balance. Two are even. Three tips on the scale. That's why a group of three women is called a coven. I have this feeling that more will be revealed once we help Otabalá. She's like the connective Spirit between the *Lwas*. I think she might be the link to the other Books. Because she's weak, we're not learning as much as we could. Everything is connected."

"The firstborn links the line," Ceres murmured, mostly to herself.

"I think who Ayizan is looking for is close too," Maggie replied, squinting as if the light started to hurt her eyes.

"You, okay?" Leatrice asked.

"Yeah, I'm fine. I guess all the wine is getting to me. I think I'll go lie down for a bit so I can be awake by lunch," getting up, Magalie said,

"Ceres?"

"Yeah?" Ceres replied, looking up at her sister. For a second, Maggie looked like she was trying to think of the right words. In the end, Maggie just shook her head,

"Nothing. I'll see you, ladies, later."

The two on the beach watched as the youngest of them walked back into the house. They were quiet for a while, watching seagulls diving into the sea, sending splashes of foaming water into the air. Finally, Ceres took a deep breath and wrapped her arms around her legs.

"Heavy," Leatrice sighed.

"Heavy," Ceres repeated. "If you don't mind me asking, how old are you?"

"Twenty-eight."

"Wow. Ph.D. and all."

"Yup."

"Heavy," Ceres replied.

Leatrice laughed.

"You know what the worst part of all of this is? I had cousins I could have been talking to all this time about all the weirdness in my life. And I didn't know about you guys,"

"And maybe I could have passed your class with a grade higher than a B,"

"Eh."

"Damn, no nepotism over here," Ceres shook her head while standing up.

"Nope, I would run you as ragged as Jean does to Philia," she chuckled, extending her arm for Ceres to take.

"Who is Philia?"

"Um, she's Jean's assistant. She's the guardian at the door if you want to get near him. The girl is twelve to fourteen hours a day in that office and is about your age. Rumor has it she's Jean's niece or something,"

A shiver moved through Ceres as they walked back to the house.

Chapter XLVII - *Damiana Leaf*

Damiana, or Feuille de Damiana, is an herb commonly found in Mexico. It is widely used by mouth as an aphrodisiac to treat sexual problems. It also treats stomach issues such as dyspepsia, diarrhea, and constipation, improving menopause and premenstrual syndrome symptoms.

In Spiritual Work: *Damiana is called the herb of love for its aphrodisiac properties. Used in love spells to attract new love or to return a straying lover. Drink a tea made of Damiana leaf to heighten sexual desire on date night.*

Getting up, Philia kissed both men on the cheeks and took the elevator upstairs. She walked as if she were going into her room, checking to ensure no one was watching her from downstairs. Then, hurried into Mateo's room, closing the door gently behind her. Philia crossed the space quickly, clicking the button on the side of the armoire to open it. The double doors slid to the sides as the shelf slid out. It was a high-tech piece of furniture made to look like an antique to not ruin the bedroom's décor.

The Xbox she was looking for was one of three game systems in the armoire. All three turned on when you pushed the power button. However, the Xbox had been gutted. It turned on, but no games were played. She went up to it and pressed a hidden button on the bottom. The system rose. Then, it opened like the jaws of a shark about to take a bite out of her hand. Her heart palpitated against her ribcage as Philia reached into the black hole. Deeper, she cautiously ventured until she was elbow-deep into it, feeling around for the large Book.

"No," Philia whispered, pulling her arm out and venturing to look inside.

Yet, her eyes didn't change what her hands felt. There was nothing there. The hiding place was empty.

"fudging fudgesicles!" She swore through gritted teeth as she closed the Xbox and the armoire.

Philia's brain went into overdrive. Maybe it was in another secret location she wasn't privy to. The idea of someone being able to walk out of this house with anything as significant as that book without Jean or Mateo's knowledge was unfathomable. The place looked innocent and pleasant but was secretly a state-of-the-art fortress guarded by modern technology.

"Magic," She spoke the word softly.

The blood drained from her face. As the realization hit her that her aunt hadn't been joking when she used to tell her that.

She was overwhelmed, completely alone, and directionless for the first time. The young woman sat at the edge of her cousin's bed and cried. The wall she had spent years carefully constructing brick by brick to hide all the emotions, fears, and loneliness behind cracked and then broke. Tears fell freely down her face faster than she could angrily wipe them away. Causing her to grow angrier that she was losing control.

Two people she had believed loved each other the way she hoped to be loved one day — and now even that seemed like a lie. She didn't know who to trust or where to turn.

When Philia was younger, she played Spy Games if she wasn't talking Mateo into a Disney princess scenario. And Uncle Jean was their unknowing, bad guy, bent on world domination. Back then, playing was more accessible than the Little Mermaid since he was always dressed in fancy suits, constantly on the phone, and flew off to different places. Philia could remember following him around, taking pictures of him doing secret handshakes. It had been amusing, maybe even welcomed. It was undoubtedly great summer fun for her, but now, without her "big brother" for backup, it wasn't a game she wanted to play.

Philia fell back onto the bed, wiping away her tears. On the ceiling was a mural. Esperanza hired a painter to create it for Mateo when she got so sick that she could hardly speak. In Esperanza's letters to him explaining the mural, she said she wanted him to remember the story to tell his little girl one day. The mural was not very old and featured what the family called The Great Escape. It was a fable about how the daughters of one of the High Priestesses escaped the fire at the Great Library. Four dark-haired women carried scrolls in the painting as they ran away from a massive building on fire. The scrolls contained knowledge given to them by their mother, a woman as old as this world.

Two figures stood before the building; its Roman columns were beset by flames. The woman was wearing a white dress with a delicate crown on her head. Long locks of grey hair had grown around the coronet and intertwined with the silver headpiece. The man was wearing a yellow ankle-length skirt with a golden helmet.

A beam of light seemed to run from the tip of his helmet's peak to the sky. It pierced the parting clouds. His arm stretched upwards as if pleading to be received. No one knew the woman or man's name or why the fable was important. Nevertheless, the mural was an exceptional work of art paid handsomely for, and the attention to detail showed precisely what people meant by *'you get what you pay for.'*

It was the first time Philia had seen this painting like this. Typically, if Philia were here around this time, Mateo would be in his room also. She was surprised by the new details she spotted now that she was alone to study it. Details like the way the gold shined. The colors of the women's eyes. Even some writing on the scrolls. Philia sat up to take a better look. Her brown eyes scan the subtle elements of the artwork. The young woman was just about to stand on the bed when the sound of the door swinging open wider got her attention.

Philia turned in that direction and froze. The old woman she'd seen in the window earlier stood at the door, staring silently at her. The woman was oddly dressed in thin white fabric layered on each other, resembling a toga and a jumpsuit mixture, with the lower part of her face covered by a veil secured by a silver circlet. *She's not a cleaner*, Philia thought.

"Hello," She called out softly as she sat up, wondering how the solid oak door was opened in the first place without her hearing it.

It wasn't the kind of door that would mistakenly stay open when you thought you closed it. It was heavy, and you heard the sound when it closed. It had been closed; Philia was sure of it. Yet, she was sure she hadn't heard it open, only widening. She looked down for a second, and the woman was gone.

The young woman sauntered to the door and looked into the hall. No one was there, but a light was on in the library.

Maybe she was in there? She thought *perhaps it was one of Jean's friends that she didn't know was coming over and got lost.* Her uncle had many unique friends with a particular sense of fashion.

Of course, She reasoned.

"Hello," She called out softly, walking towards the library.

Philia knew the men were still downstairs since she could hear the echo of their voices from up there. She walked through the hall with a glass wall, tracing her fingers over the protective magical sigils etched in the windows separating the library from the bedroom. Esperanza had confided the truth to Philia. She had felt disturbed when Jean started collecting certain esoteric items. Although Jean had assured Esperanza that they were safe. She hadn't felt safe. So, she found a glass artist and made Jean hire him the next day to put the sigils up for the family's safety.

hilia had watched enough movies and experienced one too many haunted places in France to know people believe in the occult for different reasons. At the time, Philia had reasoned with her aunt's failing health. Yet, Esperanza felt comforted by these symbols. Until Mateo's messages, as Philia touched the glass, she hoped to glean some new understanding. She was only a few feet from the library's doors when she saw the tail end of the old woman's outfit going through a row of books. The fabric looked like a trail of mist to her.

"La merde!" She swore softly as she stopped, suddenly aware she might be chasing a ghost. But like in the movies, these sigils did nothing to keep Spirits out.

"Never works for the dead, never. The only evil things that are still breathing," Philia confirmed with a deep sigh, shaking her head,

"Why does it feel like ghosts chase me?" Philia wondered.

It's not like she had a problem with ghosts. She had become used to them over the years. Philia didn't mind the spirit. Instead of running into them, she lives and leaves those not alive alone, which was her motto.

Yup, that's all I need right now, Philia thought. *This place is haunted now and not even by my aunt.*

She fished the quartz crystal and onyx rosary from under her shirt, more for comfort than anything else. Philia held tightly to the cross as she moved forward, reciting the 'lord's Prayer.' Cautiously, she looked around the room from the open doorway. The library wasn't as extensive as it could've been. The lady of the house wanted it to seem more like a cozy reading room than a full-on library.

Accordingly, one large desk fits four people for homework or research in the middle. In addition to three comfy couches by the window and eight-foot shelves lined up along the walls opposite windows facing out to the sea. Philia quickly looked through the rows of bookcases and found nothing. Slowly moving her vision from left to right.

If she was following a ghost, she wondered, *why was it here, now?* She had never experienced any Spirit in the 20 years she had been in and out of this house.

Slowly, a vision came to the glass wall, landing on the symbol of the striped diamond with the four overextended arms and six stars around it, etched in the glass square in the middle above the couches. She stared in confusion at it for a moment.

"What the hell?" she swore, surprised, moving forward. *Was that new*? She wondered.

In all the time Philia had spent in this house since the other etchings went up, she had never seen that etching before. Walking up to it, she touched it gently with the tip of her finger. She guessed it was warm from the sunlight hitting the glass. She moved closer to it to see if anything would indicate it was done recently. A spark of light in the corner of her eye caught her attention. The young woman moved towards it slowly, only to discover another etching of the same design.

"Huh,"

As she moved in to inspect this up close, another spark of light drew her farther down the wall. Curious, she followed the line until the glass ended, leaving her in a back corner with no more glass or sparks to lead her. Philia was standing in front of a section of first-edition children's books her cousin and she used to read.

Philia took a moment to clean her glasses, take a deep breath, and think. She reasoned as she put her glasses back on. There had to be a purpose behind finding herself in front of this shelf.

Everything happens for a reason, was another family motto. Although she had a distinct feeling, the reasons behind what happened would not reveal themselves quickly. She stepped back from the shelf to better view the entire thing. Before starting from the bottom left and moving up. Reading each spine on the way. Finally, with excitement and apprehension, Philia saw the same symbol on one book's spine. She pulled it out slowly just in case it was some kind of lever like she saw in the movies, which opened a hidden door or something.

When nothing happened once, she pulled it completely out. She flipped the book around in her hand in puzzlement. It wasn't a book Philia had seen before. The title was gold lettering on a white cover.

"Amore per ti," Philia read aloud, feeling the words leave her mouth like escaping vapor from a corked bottle before hearing the click of a lock behind her.

Magic word activated the hidden door, she thought triumphantly.

However, when she turned, there wasn't a hidden door. Instead, it was a drawer Philia saw sliding out from the bottom edge of the desk at the end of the rows of shelves.

Philia quickly walked over to the drawer. Maybe this was where The Book was hidden, and the ghost had been her aunt, and she just didn't recognize her. Yet as she moved closer, she quickly realized it was too small to hold The Book. Instead, Philia found a white envelope addressed to her on top of a pocket-size, wooden stash box. She was just about to open the envelope when she heard the elevator coming. Quickly stuffing the items into her pockets, Philia closed the envelope in the drawer. Then she grabbed a book from the nearby shelf and started to walk out of the library like she was reading it, meeting the others in the hall.

"Hey, I thought you were asleep," Shaka commented as he patted her.

"Not yet. I'm hoping some reading material will help,"

Shaka looked at the book's title in her hand, '*Kama Sutra: The Ancient Art of Sex Magic.*'

"Huh," He commented with wide eyes, stifling a laugh.

Philia's face turned red as she quickly pulled the book to her chest to hide the title from her uncle, who had just now reached the other two.

"Maintenant, j'ai besoin la petite sieste," Jean informed the pair, "I need more naps now at my age. My digestive properties are not what they used to be," Jean confessed coyly.

"You go ahead and take your nap, old man, but I doubt a lion's digestive properties are what yours used to be if how you eat now is any indication," Shaka replied. "I'm going to go for a run. You're welcome to join me," He offered to Philia.

"Nope," She replied without hesitation. "I'm good. I'm just going to read myself to sleep, too,"

"Happy reading," Shaka chuckled, walking off.

"What are you reading?" Jean asked curiously.

"Nothing of interest," Philia replied quickly, walking off the book at her chest.

Jean shrugged as he walked off toward his room, waving bye.

Walking into her bedroom, Philia closed and locked the door behind her. She took off her shoes and left them by the door as she jumped onto the big king-size bed and placed the book in her hand, opposite down on the nightstand. The young woman took her jacket off. Sitting in the lotus position, she pulled out the box first. The wooden container looked four-by-four and two inches deep, with a palm leaf carved into the top. It had no keyhole or indentation indicating how to open it. Still, Philia could hear something rolling inside.

Chapter XLVIII – *Dragon's Blood*

Dragon's blood has a proven healing effect on wounds, is anti-microbial, and forms a protective layer over the skin, helping keep germs away. It is anti-inflammatory and pro-collagen, making it a sought-after skincare ingredient. It is also known as an antioxidant thanks to its natural flavonoids.

In Spiritual Work: *Dragon's Blood has been used as part of rituals to neutralize negative energy. A pinch of dragon's blood increases the potency and effectiveness of other herbs in an incense mixture. Also, use it for money-drawing or love-drawing spells.*

"Leatrice, do you know if Philia Jean or his late wife's niece?"

"I'm not sure. The company is reticent about it. But, as I said, it's just a rumor."

"Philia might be the Reader. She might be one of the high Priestess."

"Really?"

"Maggie said the other Priestess might be with Jean. His niece must be it."

Leatrice said nothing for a while as they walked through the back door. Finally, she responded thoughtfully,

"If she is, what does that mean for her? I mean, you have your mother to teach you. At least to me, it feels like Philia is pretty alone here,"

"Are you guys close?"

"Not really, we hardly know each other. Still, you have to figure, a twenty-something-year-old girl that pretty, putting in those hours? That sounds like a lonely life, desperate to prove her worth to someone. I should know what I'm talking about,"

"Haitian mothers expect a lot," Ceres replied understandingly.

"Immigrant mothers," Leatrice corrected. "We have to be smarter, work harder, do better. No days off? That's not just for athletes,"

Ceres looked at her watch. It was noon; looking at the older woman's face, she smiled.

"I should have known we were family. I mean, how many Haitian people have green hazel eyes like ours? We should have known. We were from the same stock," Leatrice jokes,

"Well, you're not a geneticist, and we didn't spend that much time around each other. Plus," Ceres confessed, going to the refrigerator for a drink as Leatrice sat down,

"My mom confessed that Gerda asked her not to say anything to us; she wanted you to stay focused on your work and get your doctorate. My mom did say she asked your mom to keep an eye on you in case anything manifested,"

Leatrice thought she never told her mom about her experiences with the elements. Her mother had watched her start researching Spiritualism and the Orisha, yet they never spoke about it. The cross was still above the dining room table in her mom's house. They still prayed and went to church most Sundays.

"So, do I have to do an initiation thing?" She asked sarcastically.

"Shit!" Ceres exclaimed, popping up from her position in front of the fridge. "You do,"

"What? I was joking."

"But we have to wait till the next full moon, I'm thinking,"

"No, we don't, and we can't. We will do a proper one for everyone, including you, on the next full moon. But Leatrice should at least dream-walk to bind with Spirit," Diana chimed in while coming down the stairs, stopping to stretch midway; she walked over to Leatrice, hugging her tightly.

"I thought the Dream-walk was the initiation?" Ceres questioned her mother, telling Leatrice how sorry they were for not telling them the truth sooner.

Kissing Leatrice on both cheeks, Diana sat next to the young doctor.

"It's a large part of it, not all of it; first, you Dreamwalk; second, you bind to Spirit; then finally, you pledge your guardianship and fidelity in continuing the distribution of the Knowledge. It's not a huge thing to do the first two parts out of order, and the three of you can do the last part together, your mom, too, if she chooses. Although Gerda is not part of the bloodline, she is Haitian, so her ancestral ties should be strong." Diana took Leatrice's hand into hers. "I'm truly sorry we kept so much from you,"

"Uh-huh." Ceres cleared her throat.

"Guys, from you guys. Plural," Diana corrected, rolling her eyes at her daughter as Ceres came to sit with them. "I want to use the excuse that between everything happening with your dad and my brother, things got complicated, but it's a bullshit excuse,"

"I'm sorry for your loss, too," Leatrice squeezed her hand, giving her a gentle smile.

"Well, anyway," Diana continued, clearing her throat as she pushed back some tears, "your mom is on her way, and when she gets here, we'll do a Dreamwalk with you before we start getting ready for lunch,"

"Mom, lunch is in less than two hours. So, this is a bad idea," said the young Priestess.

"She's not a Reader. Nevertheless, Leatrice should at least bind with her Spirit before this lunch starts. At least that way, she'll have some added protection from the ancestors, just in case Jean is the bad guy in all of this,"

"Alright, mom, but Leatrice is already tired. We're all tired. We won't finish everything on time, even if we just do a binding; we would be jumping ahead, binding her with her Spirit, which she does not know. So, let's just do a Spiritual Awakening first. That should be the first step, done the first full moon, after a young woman's first règ,"

Diana looked at her daughter in confusion.

"You probably don't remember because you didn't do one for Magalie or me. For the same reason, I'm guessing you kept a lot of information about The Book from us. Instead, you gave us the protection baths," Ceres continued, answering her mother's unspoken question and looking at Leatrice. Ceres explained,

"Think of it as a meet and greet. With that other voice in your head, that's not your voice but the voice of your soul Spirit. Which is your connection to the eternal. You take a simple tea made of Mugwort, Valeriana officinalis, African dream herb, Lemon balm, and Intellect plant. Go to sleep, have a dream, and shake hands. I got it from The Book, something my mother should have done for us."

"Yes, of course, I remember something else I regret. Alright, we'll awaken both mother and child," Diana decided. Standing up, she hugged Ceres before going into action to collect the herbs in the kitchen.

As if on cue, the front door beeped, and Gerda walked into the house with arms loaded with groceries.

"I thought we were going shopping together?" Diana asked, rushing to her side to help.

"We were, but I passed this farmer's market I had never seen before on my way back. Something made me stop. Suddenly, I was buying pomegranates, apples, Cornish hens, and saffron. I had a vision of the whole meal and knew exactly what we were cooking,"

Ceres pulled a bouquet from one of the bags she had taken from Gerda. It was a gorgeous arrangement of twelve long-stemmed white roses interlaced with baby's breath against a royal palm piece backing.

"Nice centerpiece," Ceres admired, showing it to her mother.

"Yeah, this old lady in a white dress just gave them to me. I had so many bags that she had moved on when I found money to give her. I looked for her, but she was gone. I guess she must have gone into one of the adjacent stalls," Gerda told them, all smiles.

"How much coffee did you drink when you got home?" Leatrice asked her mother, taking things into the kitchen.

"I didn't have any coffee. After I packed something for you to wear, I had a cup of tea, lit some candles, and took a shower. I must have fallen asleep because I had the most interesting dream. I was sitting in bed wearing a white dress and white *mouchwa* when this beautiful glowing angel with large white wings walked up to the front of my bed and asked me if I was ready. When have I asked, ready for what? He touched me in the center of my forehead and vanished. I woke up feeling clear and focused, dressed, and now I'm here."

"What kind of tea?" Ceres asked suspiciously.

"I don't know. It was something Magalie gave me before I left,"

"Of course," Ceres concluded. Her sister had beaten them to the punch.

"Well, I guess that took care of itself," Diana stated, looking at the glow about Gerda. "Gerda, let's start with lunch, and I'll explain your dream. Then, Leatrice, go upstairs and shower while we start some tea. You'll need to be cleansed of negative energy for this next part. After that, Ceres will bring you some candles." Diana finished placing a tea kettle on the stove.

The Book had opened when Diana checked for inspiration, revealing Persian roasted hens with saffron, lemon, and garlic — the answer to her unspoken question:

'What's for lunch?'

Gerda was glad she had received the information from the Spirit for something that sounded fancy yet made the oven do most of the work. Since baking something in the oven was precisely the amount of conscious thought-processing power, she felt she could give anything right now. The house smelled of Asian spices they had roasted earlier in the saucepan before dressing the hens.

Gerda was sitting at the bar next to Magalie, breaking apart pomegranates. Some seeds were added to the sangria, while others were added to a chocolate mousse dessert Diana made.

"I just noticed that many of the ingredients you're using for the mousse are very similar to those of a love spell," Gerda chuckled.

"Anytime you're working on getting something from someone, whether it's truth, favor, or compliance, you should always add a bit of love to it," Diana winked at her from inside the kitchen,

"Love is what opens our Spirit to possibilities, to seeing the good in people, to wanting and willing, to help others, and be better people ourselves," Diana informed the two at the kitchen bar.

"I know, mom," Magalie affirmed.

"Repetition is the key to learning it in the bones," Diana confirmed.

Magalie had come down about 30 minutes ago, very relaxed, yawning, and stretching until she came face to face with her perturbed mother and older sister. As well as a very jubilant and refreshed Gerda.

"I was going to do the same thing," Ceres started, "but at least I had the decency to tell Leatrice what I wanted to do. And didn't just send her home with a bag of tea and tell her to take this, and it'll help her sleep!"

"I didn't tell her it would help her sleep. I think I just said, ``Here, have some tea when you get home," The young woman answered with a wry smile, trying to gauge the anger her elders had towards her at this point.

"Seriously, Mom," Ceres sucked her teeth, shaking her head at her little sister. In annoyance or irritation, Magalie wasn't sure.

Chapter XLIX – *Wormwood*

Wormwood is an herb that can be used in supplement form. Potential benefits include symptom relief for Crohn's disease, aid with digestion, and lower arthritis pain. It also has antioxidant benefits.

In Spiritual Work: *A powerful apotropaic herb, which means that it protects from evil. Legend holds that Wormwood planted around your garden will keep pests and snakes away. It can be used for boundary magick and is burned in incense designed to aid in developing psychic powers and can also be worn for this reason. Carry it with you to protect you from bewitchment.*

She put the box down and picked up the envelope with her name on it. The handwriting on it was that of her Aunt Esperanza. Her script was very distinctive, with the flair of a noble French woman, with the capital letters of each sentence dancing to the occupying word.

"Ma petite Phil,

There were so many things that I wished we had the time to discuss when we were together. I hope you know how much I love you. And how much you being here meant to me; you are the daughter I never had. You come from some great women; Marie Izabella, your mother, is as exceptional as any person before her. And now, you will carry the torch. I wish we had more time together, more time alone. If you're reading this letter, it means I'm gone, and so has your mother, leaving you alone to carry this burden because only you can.

My beautiful Mateo may be able to help you, but I'm afraid this is your charge to have. So here I am, writing this letter, unable to speak, feeling the life force draining slowly from me, and scared to trust anyone else with this information. In writing this, I have come to fear the person I once loved most. Be very cautious of your uncle.

Philia read that last line three times and felt her heartbreaking anew each time. The world she knew and had felt safe in all these years was shattering. And a part of her refused to accept that it was true. Jean told her that her aunt had been very sick, even paranoid. Taking a deep breath and swallowing hard, she kept reading.

You found me on the balcony crying on the night of your sixteenth birthday at the Gala with your mother and father here. When we spoke, I told you I had many regrets. I was so close to telling you the truth, but I couldn't say anymore when Jean showed up. He didn't want me to give you the gift I planned to give you that night. Returning to you what was rightfully yours as the first daughter of our family, The Book. He had become obsessed, and I was too blind to see.

You have to understand, ma Cherie, I took The Book before I knew its true purpose. We were young and in love, and after we ran away, I spent years disconnected from my family. Unable to face your mother's disappointment or your mother's sorrow. It was about 3 years when we started making real money, and I started sending money back home. And a year later, I felt comfortable reaching out to my family.

I was horrified to learn that my father had passed, and although your mother said she sent letters, I never received them. Jean and I assumed they must have gotten lost while we were moving. We moved a lot then. Jean needed his surroundings to reflect his position.

When I finally got back in touch with my mother, she refused to speak unless I came home with The Book. Ta mère knew our newly found luck had to do with The Book. Isabella warned me about using The Book's knowledge to gain wealth. As we did, it would ultimately be detrimental to us. Everything came at a cost, your mother insisted. That was why women were the Readers. They were less likely to be selfish and use it correctly for the benefit of the community.

Some part of me knew it was my mother's words that were coming true. Otherwise, why else hadn't our family used it like Jean and I were? Making money quickly instead of choosing to scrape by while keeping The Book unharmed during the war. But I was young and dismissed it as an old mentality that belonged to the ancient world. In America, people used whatever was to their advantage to make money with no consequence.

Instead of stopping, I tried harder to help Jean see the writing of The Book, something he barely could do in the first place. I hope that getting him to read it would prove that part of my mother's warning was wrong. But, then maybe, all of it was wrong. He started becoming suspicious of me when it didn't work for him. Perhaps Jean thought I was holding things back from him to control him, but that wasn't it.

A couple of aged wet spots down the letter made Philia realize her aunt had been crying when she wrote this letter, almost bringing tears to her eyes. But she fought them back.

I loved him more than the world. I wanted a big family with him, daughters, and sons to carry on the Dieudonne name. But that wasn't meant to be. Soon, my mother's prediction started to pass; one child after another, healthy for six to seven months. Then, dying inside of my womb for reasons no doctor could determine.

You see, there is a natural energy flow. A natural flow to the way the knowledge in The Book works. When you use what's in it to help those around you, what you want will naturally flow toward you, and the energy from those who benefited from those good deeds flows back into The Book to strengthen it. But instead, Jean and I only used it for our gain, and as it was not getting any outside energy from us, it started draining me as its only source.

By the third stillbirth, I was determined to stop. We were already millionaires, and I didn't think more money was as important as a family of our own. Moreover, Jean was on the rise and had made some powerful friends. He knew ancient remedies not readily available to the public. And he insisted those men could help. At first, I thought it was a miracle that Jean had received the potion, which allowed us to have

Mateo, but only Mateo, as the next child, was a stillbirth.

I begged him for more of the potion. I wanted more children. I wanted a daughter of my own. Yet, he insisted he couldn't get more. He refused to tell me where it came from or who made it. Now I know the potion was a *cheval de Troie* — a curse wrapped as a gift. Given to him by people searching for our family's Book, I'm not certain for what purpose. They are dangerous, Phil. These people should never get The Book.

I've asked Mateo to hide The Book, but I haven't told him everything I think I know. Unfortunately, his anger towards his father might cause him to reveal things he should not.

Phil, The Book is yours. You are the only first-born female of this generation. I should be there to properly entrust this to you. But I'm not. I apologize to you for this. As your twenty-second birthday approaches, I wouldn't be surprised if something regarding The Book brings you home. I'm going to need you to trust me. In the box that should be with this letter is a vial. After you shower, light three white, yellow, and green candles, dress in white, and drink the tonic. I will speak to you in your dreams.

My love always,

Philia reread the letter for instructions on how to open the box. But there were none. She frowned and picked up the box again, tracing the leaf with her fingertips. As Philia outlined it, it felt like one of the leaves moved down under pressure. She stopped and pushed it again with purpose this time. The palm frond moved in, and the top separated into two parts, revealing the little bottle inside. Philia slowly took it out. She held it to the light. It was a small, clear bottle with a cork stopper. Judging by the way the liquid inside gently cascaded down the walls of the container, in nature, it was alcoholic. Maybe a tincture, a concoction made by diluting plants in an alcohol solution. Her mother used to make those to help neighbors with ailments.

Well, a shot of alcohol will help her get some sleep, she thought.

Philia got up from the bed and went to her armoire. She pushed a button, and it opened up like her cousin's. Instead of game systems, two small chests appeared. She opened the one to the right where she kept her meditation accouterment, pulling out the three colored candles as her aunt had instructed.

Philia arranged the candles on the nightstand next to her bed. She sat there for a minute, looking at the vial. Philia trusted her aunt and knew Esperanza would never hurt her.

Nevertheless, the cautious Philia still felt she should tell someone she was about to drink a foreign substance with unknown side effects. But she knew she couldn't. So, placing the vial next to the candles, Philia headed into her ensuite bath.

Out of the bathroom, Philia dressed for a nap in a white T-shirt, panties, and bra. She walked to the candles and lit them. Philia made sure to keep her thoughts on her aunt's loving face. Taking the vial into her hand, she twisted the cap off and drank the contents. The liquid was pungent and sweet, burning her chest on its way down. The letter had not given her any words to say. Yet, Philia thought about it and felt like words needed to be said. Closing her eyes, Philia repeated the invocation that her aunt had taught her so long ago.

"May the God who created me take my hand, direct the breath of my mouth, and lead my feet where I may manifest my birthright."

Philia wasn't sure what she was expecting as the tonic took hold of her, and she tried to drift off to sleep. After a few minutes of tossing and turning, she decided to give up and that getting ready for lunch would be a better use of her time. Standing up, she moved her legs across the bed and thought she had planted them firmly on the floor but soon realized that she was ethereal. She looked back on the bed and saw her body lying there, calmly asleep. The scene changed. Philia found herself in a familiar place, the library of her uncle's house. Esperanza was sitting on one of the sofas. The vial of tonic Philia had taken and a box on her lap. Esperanza appeared to be waiting for her.

Esperanza looks older, Philia thought, *even older than when she passed.*

Her hair, which had always been arranged in lovely grey curls around her face, was thinning, and her face was even more sunken than Philia remembered.

Was that possible, she wondered?

Esperanza's mouth curved into a smile; Philia could see the corners trembling as if the effort to hold it was too much. She wore the green satin dress with the lace overlay that ran up her neck, which Jean had buried her in. She motioned Philia to come and join her on the sofa.

As Philia sat beside Esperanza, she wondered why her aunt hadn't spoken. Esperanza leaned in as if she was about to hug her niece. Instead, she placed the fingers of her right hand on the base of Philia's skull. The young woman jolted upright both physically and spiritually. Her mouth widened as if something locked inside her was being released.

The scene changed.

Now, Philia was in the hospital bed with her aunt. Esperanza was very weak and on the brink of death. Jean was there, apologizing to her about how he'd failed her. Philia felt his presence more than she saw him. She was experiencing things from her aunt's point of reference. In her mind, Philia heard the soft voice of her aunt in her French accent saying,

"*I am too weak to speak to you, but now that I have brought you into the Spirit world, I can show you as much as possible by opening up the energy base of your skull called the Alta Major. Our divine connection to God, the breath of life, is where your soul and Spirit lie. I will show you what I can, but I am too weak to maintain this connection for long. As my Spirit is not at rest and I have yet to join the ancestor,*"

"What does that mean?" Philia asked, but no answer came.

She felt other presence in the hospital room, but she wasn't sure how many. Then she heard a voice. "*We can still stop this if we can find the means to read The Book. It'll go faster with your son.*"

"*Never,*" she heard Jean say forcefully, interrupting the other man speaking.

"*Well then, you must find Shaka Solomon and get close to him* by any means. *We need fresh blood to keep reading his Book for more information that might help,*" another voice advised.

"Oh my god, is Shaka being used too?" Philia asked, but again, no answer came.

The scene changed. Esperanza stood against a wall in a white silk night robe — younger but still frail, grey curls falling around her face. She was listening to Jean on the phone, her expression carefully still.

"She is fading fast, and nothing I have done has worked. I still cannot read The Book without her!" He yelled in frustration, slamming his hand flat on The Book, sitting next to the griddle on the marble countertop. *"And reading it with my son has proven pointless over the years. You assured me that my bond through him would strengthen my relationship with The Book.*

The scene changed again. Esperanza was a young waitress, stylish and slender in her twenties, and she was wearing a red knee-high dress with a striped collar and cuffed sleeves, wiping down the counter in front of a younger Jean. She was speaking in French.

"Last night, when we were conversing about your frustrations at work, I opened The Book, and the page that came up said, 'true wealth comes from doing what you can, when you can, where you can, even when you don't feel like doing it.'"

From where Philia was observing, she could see Jean's brown leather jacket and white shirt as he ran his fingers through his hair. He was looking at the front page of *The New York Times*.

There was a big picture of a wealthy French millionaire, André Benoît Mathieu Meyer.

Jean wasn't reading it.

"*And you take that to mean that we should go to work today, even though I don't feel like it.*"

"*Yes,*" she confirmed, kissing him on the cheek. "*It's not like I can go gallivanting with you for free stuff. I just started this job. We need money.*"

As she spoke, the door to the restaurant opened, and a rain-soaked older gentleman walked in, removing his hat and shaking the water off his dark coat.

"*Mon Deux, the papers said it was a good day to walk.*"

As he spoke, Esperanza looked down at the paper and realized it was the man from the front page.

The scene changed again, but things were not as sharp as before.

"*I cannot hold this connection much longer,*" she heard the voice of Esperanza say.

Now Philia found herself in another familiar place, her parents' bookshop in France, with a young Jean and Esperanza. Jean was excitedly pacing in front of Esperanza, sitting on the floor with The Book open.

Jean was asked,

"*How did it know Mrs. Pierre would pay me extra?*"

"*I don't know. It didn't say that exactly. It's just how I interpreted it.*"

"*That is the third time in a row. I've been paid the highest amount for my work,*" Jean chuckled, kissing her.

Philia could feel how much her aunt loved him.

"*Are you sure there is nothing you can interpret about turning aluminum into gold?*" Jean asked softly.

"*Something that can make a man like me wealthy enough to be worthy of a woman as beautiful as you?*"

Philia could feel intense desire from Esperanza rising as she was about to answer. Just then, Philia's grandmother came into view. The caramel-skinned woman was wearing a black dress, and her hair was in a tight ponytail. She looked at Jean, then at The Book in Esperanza's hands, and anger flashed across her face as she started yelling.

In Spanish, Philia thought, but the vision was fading. In what Philia believed was her aunt's last bit of strength, she heard her say,

"*Keep The Book away from Jean.*"

Philia woke up with a start. She was breathing heavily, and her heart was racing. She had been bombarded with so much information she didn't know where to start. Then, finally, her aunt's last words repeated in her head.

Keep The Book away from Jean.

Yet Philia couldn't. She didn't even know where it was, and Jean was already searching for it with more help than she had. Then, finally, a moment of absolute clarity overcame her; Philia had to prevent Leatrice from telling him anything she had learned. In a panic, Philia jumped off her bed and searched her cell phone.

Chapter L - *Comfrey*

Comfrey is also known as Boneset, Black roots, Black wort, Bruisewort, or Knit bone. Comfrey is a tea for upset stomachs, ulcers, heavy menstrual periods, diarrhea, bloody urine, persistent cough, painful breathing, bronchitis, cancer, and chest pains.

In Spiritual Work: *Comfrey is used magically for health, healing, protection during travel and prosperity. Keep a satchel with comfrey on your person when traveling to keep you safe, or place some in your luggage to protect it from being stolen.*

"Mags, you know you just can't do things like that. What if she had a bad reaction? Gerda was home alone,"

"In my defense. I gave Gerda the tea before I knew Leatrice would stay behind. Honestly, I can't remember. I'm sorry, Mrs. Gachette," Magalie offered sincerely.

"I'm fine," Gerda shouted, "look at me, I'm great! It's all worked out. You're always saying everything happens for a reason, Dee. Well, we were short on time," The older woman rushed over, dragging each woman into her embrace. They were all intertwined in a big group hug, and Ceres headed upstairs to tend to Leatrice.

The youngest of them was sitting next to Gerda. Explaining to her the rudimentary points of the soul and Spirit. The way she knew it versus what happened during the Awakening.

"Everyone is born from Spirit, but not everyone has a soul," Gerda repeated slowly, her brain reaching for connective threads.

"If you think of Spirit, like a spark fire that starts life. Then, the soul is the flame that grew from that spark," Maggie said, eating another piece of bread and making a puppy face at her mother. "I'm starving," she whined,

Diana pursed her lips at her daughter, opening the oven to look at the baking hens. The fowls had only begun to turn a slight brown as fat pimpled over their skin,

"Still not ready," she advised her daughter with a smirk while she closed the door, "just keep eating your Cuban bread. That's a perfect metaphor," Diana informed her daughter.

"I'll have to remember it next time. I'm trying to explain the soul to someone,"

"It is," Gerda agreed, "So, the more time and effort you put into the strengthening of your connection to God, the stronger your soul gets,"

"Yeah, kinda, I don't like to say, God. People always follow religious rules when you say the G-word," Maggie said hesitantly.

"Close enough," Her mother agreed.

"And a strong enough soul," Gerda continued, "can manifest itself outside of you,"

"Yes," both Bastille women agreed this time.

"Because we are of mind, body, and Spirit,"

"Yes," again, in unison,

"Therefore, we do an Awakening as a means of a conscious introduction between mind and Spirit. So that people don't panic when this type of Spirit manifestation happens. The man of my dreams–I mean, in my dreams–is my Spirit, and I shouldn't tell anyone the name he told me."

"Yes," Diana confirmed, "Not that you will be able to. I've tried, and it turns into one of those things that's on the tip of your tongue, but you can't remember."

"He is the man of your dreams, too," Maggie said with a wink, her mother shaking her head disapprovingly.

"Our soul's name is our most secret possession and should never be spoken to anyone else," Gerda continued, repeating the information she had just learned.

"Exactly, unless you want someone or something calling your Spirit away from you while you're asleep," Diana warned her with a smirk.

"Is that real?" Gerda asked with a look of concern.

"I don't know, it's an old saying, but I don't want to find out, do you?" Her friend asked with a raised eyebrow.

"This is a lot of fudging information," Gerda conceded.

"Yes," the other two women agreed, busting out laughing.

"It'll get easier," Ceres said, returning down the stairs.

"Is everything okay?" Gerda asked, getting up. Ceres waved her to sit back down.

"She's fine. She's just waking up. I'm sure you guys will have a lot to talk about when she comes downstairs,"

"Like what?"

"No idea," Ceres shrugged. "The soul Spirit hotties, maybe," She winked at Gerda, making the older woman blush. "No, but seriously, when is lunch? I'm starving, this day is draining, and it's not even halfway done,"

Diana washed her hands and left the kitchen to take Ceres' hand.

"Come sit," Diana offered her daughter a seat on the floor as she sat on the couch behind her. "Take off your shoes and relax," She directed Ceres as she closed her eyes.

Breathing deeply with her hands in a prayer position. Slowly, the older Priestess spread her hands apart over her daughter's head, with her palms facing up. As Diana breathed, she imagined her body was a glowing being made of light floating in a lotus position through clouds of infinite chaotic energy.

They flowed like lightning bolts, streaming quickly past her in fuchsia pink, electric blue, sunrise yellow, and blinding white, waiting. The creative energy with no mind, no consciousness, no reason of its own. Able to be used for good or evil, heal or hurt. By whoever has the knowledge of how to tap into it.

Diana released a long breath while lovingly placing both hands on her daughter's shoulders. She imagined herself calling the open-source energy to flow into her. At the same time, she saw it flow through her fingertips and into her daughter. Within moments, Ceres' breathing was synchronized with her mother's.

On the receiving end, Ceres could feel the warmth of the energy flowing through her mother.

"This kind of energy healing is called Reiki," Diana said, not opening her eyes.

"It doesn't drain me, as it helps Ceres. When done correctly, Reiki helps both the giver and the receiver. As the energy passes through one person and into another. I learned about it from a Japanese healer. I think it is important for people to learn all aspects of energy use; the more we learn, the more tools we have at our disposal, and the less afraid we will be of each other,"

Diana had taught the girls that the Tree of Life had infinite branches. '*With roots so deep, that one would have to be a complete idiot to ever believe they knew anything with absolution,*'

It was with this openness to different forms of healing. Ceres had started medical school. The same receptivity allowed her to see the symptoms of illness differently from her peers, which got her high marks. Finally, Diana opened her eyes and squeezed Ceres' shoulders. The young Priestess took a deep breath and exhaled, standing up to stretch.

"Maman, you're the best,"

"My turn," Maggie called out, standing up.

"Nope," Diana said, "maybe later. We two should take showers and purify ourselves of any lingering negative energies we picked up today. It's half-past twelve, and lunch is at two,"

Leatrice, now fully awake, walked downstairs into the kitchen.

"You, okay?" Gerda asked, getting down from her seat to hurry over, a look of concern on her face.

"I'm okay. My mind is spinning, but physically, I'm good,"

Taking her daughter into her arms, Gerda hugged Leatrice tightly.

"Nothing we can't handle, my dear," Gerda assured her.

Leatrice pulled away from her mother with a smile.

"As long as we're together," she confirmed, kissing Gerda.

"O.m.g, they are so cute," Magalie commented.

"Shower!" Gerda reminded her firmly in her motherly voice.

"Alrighty, lady, geez."

"Auntie!" her mother called after her, causing Ceres to snicker.

"Mothers. Saving the world while parenting our kids, all at once," Gerda commented.

"I wish we could pause time, read minds, and all that jazz," Diana jokes, getting up to check on the chicken again.

"Well, that blast on the beach was something," Leatrice remarked.

"Yeah, something," Ceres replied softly.

Chapter LI – *Purple Corn*

Purple corn tends to reduce blood clots, fight against hypertension, and lower blood pressure. Promotes the creation of collagen and cell renewal as well as that of connective tissues. The Anthocyanins in purple corn also help regulate and reduce cholesterol, improve blood circulation, eliminate toxins, and have an anti-inflammatory effect.

In Spiritual Work: Corn can be used in protection, luck, and divination spells. It's particularly effective when used to protect children. Simply place an ear of corn in the bed your child sleeps in. Corn is a sign of a bountiful harvest and can also be used to encourage financial prosperity.

The sudden sound of Roger Taylor, Queen's drummer, singing *Galileo...Galileo,* at a high pitch, made all the women turn towards the living room table.

"That's my phone, don't judge me!" Leatrice joked as she walked toward the music. "I left it down here when I went upstairs for my nap,"

"Okay, well, I'm glad it was on vibrate when I had it earlier," Diana quipped, "I'm going to go get cleaned up as well. Ceres, you got this?" Diana asked as she grabbed Shaka's book off the counter and headed to the stairs.

"Yes, Mom, go,"

Gerda sat on the couch, looking at her daughter thoughtfully and wondering what her experience had been like. Ceres was in the dining room, adjusting the table before the place setting, wondering who Leatrice was having a very intense conversation with. Leatrice was doing most of the listening with an intensifying look on her face, which broke every few seconds with,

"Uh-huh, I see or know what you mean."

Lunch for eight was leisurely compared to how many people their mother customarily entertained. Ceres loved to watch her mother when she hosted dinner parties. Their mother's food was always outstanding. Her charm, intelligence, and humor continuously delighted the dinner guests. The beach house was a place to enjoy good company, always without negativity. Therefore, when Diana suggested the beach house to meet Jean and Shaka for lunch. Ceres had to agree wholeheartedly.

This house was Diana's seat of her power, with all four elements at her disposal at any time. It was the safest place to be, no matter what came their way. Ceres may have been the new Priestess with unknown capabilities, but their mother was the matriarch, and she needed her mother's knowledge and strength.

The antique dining table was one of the few items left over from the late Mrs. Attiman. It was a beautiful handmade piece of furniture that could be adjusted to fit between four and fourteen people. Ceres removed the vase of roses from the center of the table, placing it on a chair in the corner so she could lift out the wooden leaf and push both ends together to shrink it. Gerda chuckled when she saw Ceres moving from one end to another, trying to make both ends come together by herself. Then, she walked over to help with a cat that ate the canary look on her face. Gerda slid over to Ceres. The young Priestess looked at Gerda suspiciously.

"You look excited,"

"It's Philia on the phone," Gerda whispered, pushing one end of the table forward.

"Who?" Ceres asked as she pushed the end of the table toward Gerda.

"Philia, Jean's..."

"Niece," Ceres finished. "Yes. What does she want?"

"From what I can gather, Philia got some kind of message from her dead aunt, Esperanza. She's not sure what's going on, but she doesn't want Leatrice to tell Jean anything she found out about the page of The Book."

"What was the message from her aunt?"

"I couldn't hear that part,"

They heard Leatrice end the call before she walked over with a very introspective look.

"I just had a fascinating conversation with Jean's niece,"

"Feel like sharing?" Ceres asked as she slid the wood slab inconspicuously behind a corner curtain.

"We're all waiting," Gerda confessed.

"It appears that Philia has been going through a mystery of her own. Philia is Jean's niece through his late wife, Esperanza. When Esperanza came to America, she brought a family heirloom, a Book of great significance that was supposed to be passed down to Philia. I'm guessing that is the book Jean supposedly lost, and we have the page here. She was rambling and sounded scared. Philia is not sure who to trust. However, she got some kind of message from Esperanza and begged me not to tell her uncle any information I might have garnered. She said she'll find a way to speak to me in private when they come for lunch,"

"So, Jean does possess one of The Books," Ceres confirmed.

"Not if what he told me about it being stolen is true," Leatrice corrected, setting some extra chairs from the dining room onto a small mat nearby.

"What about the man with Jean, Shaka Solomon? Did Philia mention him? Does he know anything?" Ceres questioned.

"No," Leatrice replied. "I mean, she didn't mention him. She may have wanted to, but she couldn't talk for long. There was a knock on her door, and she had to go quickly,"

"He doesn't," replied Diana as she descended the stairs. Her hair was wrapped in a towel. "From what I read skimming over his book, Shaka is searching for a different Book, one he believed was stolen from his tribe."

She took the towel off to let her long brown curls fall on the ankle-length, royal blue, body-hugging, short-sleeved dress she wore with strappy silver sandals. Even without makeup, the older Priestess was stunning.

"So, the plan is to make them fall in love with Diana while we drug them," Gerda teased.

"Because right now, Diana looks so good. I'm about to tell her all my secrets. Plus, give her all my money. Shit, if ageless beauty is one of y'all's powers, I will be jealous."

Diana laughed, doing a slight turn.

"No such luck, my love. However, I did leave a dress upstairs for you to change into,"

"What's wrong with what I'm wearing?" So instead, Gerda sported a perfectly tailored, dark-blue button-up shirt and black slacks.

"Very dark," Ceres answered. "Our Spirits don't deal with black, most Spiritual work doesn't deal with black, from Buddhism to Voodoo, do see people wearing black when asking for Spiritual help. Most people associate black with Spiritual work because of Hollywood movies about witchcraft. However, good or bad, real witches know the power of colors. Our family is guarded by the Spirit of Erzulie. Her colors are pink, blue, gold, and also white."

"So, does that mean I have to change too?" Leatrice asked about the white blouse and black slacks Gerda brought her from home.

"Yeah," Ceres confirmed. "Come, I think we're close enough to the same size. Although, my things will be shorter on you,"

"Just give her a dress that's not too short on you," Diana called out.

However, a very lethargic Maggie was coming down before the two could climb the stairs. Wearing a white short-sleeved t-shirt tucked into white linen cargo pants, her head was down, and it seemed like she was sleepwalking.

The groups quieted down, carefully watching her.

"Mags, are you okay?" her mother asked, walking forward, gently lifting her chin to see her face.

"Oh my god," Diana expressed in shock.

Her young daughter's pupils were dilated to the point that there seemed no irises, only the blackness beyond sight, and they were empty of any recognition.

"They attacked from the north, the Sons of Eve," The young woman began speaking in a voice entwined with a deeper trembling voice,

"They knew Lilith was there, teaching what they called blasphemy against the fundamental laws of God. The divine knowledge she had gleaned as she watched The Creator. She instructed on working with the natural energies around her to heal the sick, remain free from subjugation, and bring balance to the world through knowledge and insight. They tried to stop our mother and us from teaching our kin. But I, the eldest child, saw the attack and warned them.

Our mother sacrificed herself. As we fled to the four corners of our land with the scrolls. The Books contain all of our knowledge. Wisdom, we are now free to spread to all our bloodlines, freeing them, for all time, from subjugation."

Maggie finished, collapsing into her mother's arms, a small quartz crystal ball falling out of her hand and rolling onto the dark wood floor.

Chapter LII – *Star Fruit*

Starfruit is fiber-rich, containing around 60% cellulose, 27% hemicellulose, and 13% pectin. Starfruit includes many vitamins and minerals, including natural antioxidants such as vitamin C and gallic acid, which help prevent cellular damage.

In Spiritual Work: *Star fruit is believed to bring good luck and ward off evil. According to the principles of Feng Shui, the five-pointed stars on the skin of a star fruit represent wealth and happiness. In some cultures, Starfruits are placed near windowsills to encourage positive energy in the home.*

Ahkter and Mahkter had not even considered redoing the location spell once they were on the plane. The brothers were still drained from the invisibility spell they had cast yesterday, Ahkter, most of all. Therefore, when they returned to the jet, the brothers first showered. Significant relief for Mahkter, who was disgusted with himself for being in the same blue Armani suit for the last three days, chasing Jean Dieudonne. Before each drink, a vial of Rasayanas rejuvenation tonic.

The tonic was an Eastern Ayurvedic cocktail the brothers had brewed themselves, consisting of Shatavari, Ashwagandha, Brahmi, Tulsi, and Schisandra. They changed into casual, lightweight, all-white Sherwani suits before passing out in seats across from each other.

If Ahkter had had the vitality to follow his gut instincts when they got on the plane in the first place. And redid the location spell, the brothers would not have been surprised when they landed in Tallahassee's Million Air's private airport to find Jean's bombardier nowhere in sight.

"Merda!" Mahkter shouted as the two brothers stood in the hot sun in front of the empty bay where Jean kept his plane.

"Swearing is not going to help the situation," Ahkter informed his brother calmly.

Mahkter looked at his brother through slanted yellow eyes,

"Then, what would help the situation, dear brother?" Speaking his words almost with a hiss, "A celestial event, of unknown power and proportion, is upon us. And we're running around like rats lost in a maze, chasing after a little girl who knows nothing! May I remind you that you were the one who bound us from her with that stupid oath,"

"It was not stupid. It was honorable. We promised Jean he would be able to read The Book. He sacrificed his wife, and we were not able to hold up our end of the bargain."

"One woman's sacrifice is not worth the millions that have been sacrificed to uphold the balance as God intended."

"What does it matter now? The fact that we took his son's blood, and we're here has proven this is more important than the oath."

"It matters," Mahkter shouted, "It matters," He continued lowering his voice into a hiss as he moved closer to his brother,

"Because we should not be here. We should have taken care of the sister as soon as we found out she was pregnant instead of waiting,"

Mahkter looked like he was about to continue his rant when he paused and looked over Ahkter's shoulder. His older brother slowly turned around, following his gaze to see their pilot, waving to them as he walked in their direction.

"Señores, you have a call on the plane," the tall, dark-haired man in the black suit shouted.

Mahkter started taking hard, purposeful steps towards the jet while Ahkter took a deep breath and casually followed him. Back in the G650 and out of the sun. The headset to the phone was located in the rear of the cabin, by the sofa. It had been placed down in the center of the glass table that occupied that area. The younger of the twins picked up the receiver and positioned it so that both brothers could listen to the other end simultaneously.

"Etiam," Mahkter greeted in Latin.

"Excusatio ob interpellatam," The male voice on the other end advised, asking to pardon his interruption,

"Gentlemen, you are needed back in the rectory right away. Something is happening with The Book of the Ashanti tribe," The caller advised in a thick accent. Then, without saying another word, the other line ended the call. The brothers said nothing to the pilot, who was already pulling up the hatch door in preparation for the jet to head back east over the Atlantic Ocean.

Chapter LIII - *Aloe*

It has antioxidant and antibacterial properties to accelerate wound healing. It reduces dental plaque and treats canker sores. In addition, it relieves constipation and may improve skin and prevent wrinkles.

In Spiritual Work: *Lore states that growing an aloe plant in your house will help prevent household accidents, mainly burns. In Africa, aloe plants hang over doors to bring luck and destroy evil.*

If all spells worked, as well, this truth spell was working. I need to spend more time with the paternal side of my family, Leatrice thought.

In the first pour of the sangria, everyone had a glass. Jean toasted his newfound friends and the Gods for providing him a way to have one more glimpse of his wife's youthful face, even if it was through a surrogate.

"Well, my face isn't going anywhere for a while, God willing," Gerda jokes, "and as today has proven, we never really know what's in store for us; I'm sure we'll see each other after lunch,"

Leatrice used Jean's distracted state to sneak into the kitchen with Philia. The two tried to exchange information about what was happening between the two separate groups as quickly and quietly as possible.

"A lot is happening, I mean, a lot. I doubt we'll have enough time right now to go over everything before people start getting suspicious," Leatrice whispered, looking over her shoulder at the lively group in the living room.

"I know!" Philia exclaimed a little louder than she wanted to, quickly covering her mouth with both of her hands as she brought her voice down to a whisper,

"I mean, I'm still trying to connect everything cohesively," Philia continued, picking up her phone off the counter. So she could pretend to be scrolling.

"Yeah, my brain is more fried from the last 3 days than when I was working on my thesis. Oh," Leatrice remembered, "Don't drink the sangria. It's a truth serum."

"No way," Philia mouthed, her eyes going wide.

"Yeah, it was the fastest way we could think of to get everything out. Please trust me when I tell you we must get everything out fast."

"Why? What's happening? Are we up against a deadline or something?" Philia looked concerned.

"I think there are some things the Bastilles have to speak about themselves. But just know, you and that Book are critical. So, we need to get it back to you ASAP."

Philia looked terrified as Leatrice spoke, compelling the older woman to put an arm around her.

"It's going to be okay. I know you don't know us. Shit, I just found out the Bastilles are my cousins," The doctor chuckled wryly, shaking her head in disbelief,

"But I promise you, you are not alone in this," She finished, pulling her into a tight hug.

While in the living room, Gerda poured Jean another glass of sangria, as Diana suggested very sweetly to Shaka,

"A man like yourself deserves to taste my country's award-winning rum. Barbancourt is not easy to get hold of here. I only offer it to special guests."

By that time, the ladies had brought lunch to the table. Each guest received a Cornish game hen on their plate, with a side of rosemary roasted, rosette white potatoes. Jean was on his third glass of sangria, telling Gerda about his exploits with Esperanza in between bits of food. How two kids, madly in love, ran away to a far-off land to make their fortune. With the help of an old book, which may or may not be magical.

"This is one of the best meals I've had," Jean paused to compliment Diana.

Everyone at the table nodded in agreement as they quietly ate while listening and dissecting Jean's words.

"People like me think magic is these big things you see in the films, with sparks, fire, and levitation," Jean continued as Magalie chuckled at that, causing her mother to give her a stern look. Jean, however, continued without noticing,

"Mais réalité, it is as simple as knowing where to be, to meet the right person. Like dinner the other night," Jean concurred while raising his glass to the table before taking another drink.

Gerda chuckled beguilingly beside him as she refilled Jean's glass with more sangria.

"So, were you showing up at the restaurant part of your book's magic last night? Did it tell you to go there?" Gerda asked with flirtatious skepticism as she gently touched Jean's hand on the table.

Earlier in the day, Diana and Ceres instantly saw an opportunity when they saw Jean's reaction to Gerda descending the stairs. Pulling her to the side, Diana handed the pitcher of sangria and said,

"You will be more charming than you have ever been in your life. But you will question him like he is some guy you have a bad feeling about, trying to take Leatrice out, and you're trying not to piss off Leatrice,"

Gerda had used all her strength to not bust off laughing from the instruction as she took the pitcher in her hand, and Ceres rolled her eyes at her mother.

"Yes and no," Jean replied, taking another sip. "I used a technique Zaza had taught me from The Book. It allows the connection to what I want to pull me towards it by focusing on it. Zaza said that everything anyone ever wants was in the Universe already in existence. The money, cars, houses, whatever it was, my obtuse mind could imagine was there. The problem is that we don't know how to connect to it.

We lack the mental focus that's needed to draw it to us. Because no one ever really stops to think about what the person wants. People say they want to be rich. There are trillions, billions, and gazillion dollars in the world, waiting for someone to claim it. Rich is *relatif,* a different number for everybody. You have to know what your number is,"

The old man informed the table sternly before taking another drink from his glass.

"Last night, however," He paused thoughtfully, "I was not looking to go to the restaurant. I was in search of something else, and it led me there. So maybe I got what I wanted without knowing. That's what I wanted," He looked at Gerda with a smile that quickly faded as his eyes darted across the table to his niece.

"Pardon, mon Philia." As he cleared his throat, Jean advised regretfully, "We don't discuss The Book outside of the family," He informed Gerda softly.

"Pas de problème uncle, it's fine," Philia instructed, mustering up a smile, "I mean, you have Leatrice researching it already, and if she trusts these women, I feel like we can trust them too,"

"Mon petit," Jean sighed deeply, lowering his eyes, "I would love to think so. I would. It is not personal, ladies," He smiled weakly, playing with the stem of the glass, "But people...." He trailed off. "You just can't trust many people with this knowledge." He took another drink, looking at Philia sadly. "I once thought I had people I could trust. I was proven very wrong at the end,"

"What people, Uncle?" His niece asked coaxingly,

"Oh, Cher," He sighed, "I met them long before you or even Mateo were born. Zaza wanted a big family, a lot of kids, to make up for the one she left behind," Jean spoke so softly that everyone on the table was trying to lean in as inconspicuously as possible to hear better,

"Zaza was 19 the first time she got pregnant...." Jean spoke about how Esperanza had been pregnant at 19.

The failed pregnancies and how he did everything he could to make her happy. As Jean spoke, the mothers in the room quickly looked at their daughters as they fought back the tears.

"By the time we made our first million, your aunt had been pregnant three or four times. Each time, we watched her belly swell with hope and prayer that this dream would finally come true, only to have the dream die inside her several months later. The first two times, I told her it had to be stress. We had moved quite a lot in those first three years," He sighed, taking a sip from his glass,

"Until the last one before Mateo, she had been on bed rest, and I'd even hired a live-in midwife to take care of her. Since I couldn't be there myself, someone had to pay the bills and build a life for our future children. At least that's what I told myself." Jean hit the table with his open hand, startling everyone,

"Pardon, pardon, I'm sorry," Jean apologized.

"It's okay, Cherie, we understand," Diana said softly, "It's good for you to get things out,"

"It is," Gerda added, squeezing the hand he had hit the table with, with a loving smile, "Keep going," She encouraged,

"Oh, Zaza," Jean said softly, swallowing hard, then reaching for another sip of sangria, "The doctors said the fetuses weren't getting enough nutrients," Jean continued, "They said it was like her body was at war with the life inside of her, taking nutrients from the babies, faster than they could absorb it." He took another sip from his glass. "Zaza took it as scientific evidence of Isabella's warning. That The Book was feeding on her,"

Across from him, Philia visibly twitched at the sound of her mother's name. Shaka and Magalie, seated on either side of her, noticed. Shaka reached over, squeezing her hand reassuringly, not moving his gaze from Jean, while Magalie leaned over and whispered,

"You can do this. More wine will help," Magalie poured more white wine into Philia's glass, which got a small smile out of her.

"That it was taking from her, for what she had denied the world," Jean scuffed, draining his cup, which Gerda quickly refilled. He clenched his jaw tightly.

"Still," Jean continued, "Esperanza would not budge. As my losses continued to grow, so did my anger and resentment toward her. Not her, so much as my inability to do it myself. You see, I learned the hard way, as a child, that I could only rely on myself!" He spoke a little louder about that lesson, "And here I was completely relying on her for information from The Book,"

Philia took a drink from her wine glass, thinking her uncle still chose his words cautiously, even under a truth serum.

To his right, Magalie sucked her teeth, rolling her eyes as she took a drink of her wine. Diana and Ceres looked at each other from opposite ends of the long table and shook their heads.

"I know Cher, I know," Jean chuckled, "mais c'est le monde. And Philia finished the wine in her glass, and Magalie quickly refilled it with an,

"Uh-huh,"

As Jean finished, Magalie took a deep breath and stood up, announcing to the table,

"I need more wine. Anyone else," Everyone raised their hands.

Diana took the opportunity to start clearing off the nearly untouched plates of food from her guests.

It was the first time, Shaka thought, *the old man hadn't complained about not finishing his food.*

Philia took a sip of wine before asking her uncle,

"Is that how you truly feel?"

"No," Jean waved his hands vigorously over the table, "Of course not, Philia. Maybe because, I was younger and foolish and didn't know better back then. But you have to understand," Jean pleaded as he reached for her hand across the table.

Chapter LIV – *Juniper Berries*

Like most other berries, they're a good source of vitamin C. Vitamin C is essential for immune health, collagen synthesis, and blood vessel function. It also acts as a potent antioxidant, protecting your cells from damage caused by unstable molecules called free radicals.

In Spiritual Work: Cleanse with juniper water by placing the object dipped in an infusion of juniper needles and left in transparent glass on the windowsill overnight so that moonlight falls on the glass. To protect the house from people with impure thoughts and from evil spirits, juniper twigs are hung on the front door.

Shaka hadn't said a word the whole time. Instead, he just kept on eating. His facial expression was tightly guarded. However, when Jean mentioned the other Book. The big man finished the last inch of the rum in his tumbler in one shot. Shaka swallowed hard as he let the heat of the alcohol sliding through his throat burn away at his compounding anger. Magalie returned to the table, stopping by Shaka to place the Barbancourt bottle before him. Before placing a bottle of white between Gerda and Diana, then finally two bottles of white in front of her and Philia.

"You're sharing, right?" Leatrice mouthed from across the table, shaking her empty glass.

Ceres and Leatrice had been listening to Jean quietly, texting each other their reaction to the story. So far, there has been a lot of OMG (oh my God), SMH (shaking my head), and GTFOHWTBS (get the fuck out of here with that BS) in their message inboxes.

Jean took the last remaining drink from his glass. As Diana came in with a new pitcher to exchange with Gerda.

"Jean, what happened next," Diana asked, sitting down, "How did your wife react to the good news?"

He chuckled sadly, shaking his head,

"You know, I didn't tell her. After all, they were the men they were because they led their families, and I wanted to be like them. So, I didn't say anything when Abdul sent me to see the twins on Canal Street,"

Diana's sudden sharp inhale during the story caught everyone's attention.

"I'm fine. I'm sorry my hand is bothering me from cooking all day," She rambled, pretending to flex her hand as she tried to stay calm at the mention of twins.

It's not a fucking coincidence, she thought, but said,

"Please, you were saying, Canal Street, I've never been there, but I have heard about it,"

Shaka quietly reached over and massaged Diana's hand on the table as Jean continued.

"I walked into something that looked like Merlin's apothecary shop straight out of a fairytale. The place seemed much bigger inside than it looked on the outside. There were jars full of dried insects, lizards, and bat-like things on shelves all over the windowless walls. Vases with glass lids holding live things like eels, toads, scorpions, and exotic, colorful plants, soaking in clear liquid, lined the single walkway that led to the back counter, where twin albino brothers stood in white lab coats."

****

Diana tried to calm her breathing at one end of the table as Mateo's words replayed in Philia's mind, "*with albino white skin and yellow eyes.*

"I was wary walking through the shop, past the vases. Then, everything just kind of flowed. I sometimes think I was in a trance when I walked through the door. And of the Great Library, which they could use to help me, but only if I was truly the leader Abdul thought I could be and was ready to make my sacrifices for the world,"

"What did The Book look like?" Shaka blurted out, bringing Jean to a complete stop.

Closing his eyes, Jean placed a trembling hand on the table. Diana put a gentle hand on the balled-up fist of the large man next to her.

"Relax," She whispered gently in his ear.

Gerda put her hand on top of Jean's hand.

"It's okay," She coaxed. "Go on,"

He turned to look at her slowly, a gentle smile crossing his tear-filled eyes. Gerda took her napkin, blotting the corners of his eyes.

"Go on," She repeated gently.

"I thought," Jean started again slowly, his voice almost in a whisper as it cracked between his words. He was only looking at Gerda now. "I thought," he paused again, tears welling in his blue eyes, "I was doing the right thing."

Gerda's eyes swelled too. She looked into Jean's tear-filled eyes. Diana reached over to her friend, patting her back for strength. Magalie reached over and put an arm around Philia, sitting beside her, whose energy she could feel was in turmoil.

"I told her it was a new experimental medicine...." He paused again, hanging his head as he continued to speak.

"And put The Book back in its place."

Next to Diana, Shaka tensed up as if he was about to interrupt again. Diana, who was still holding his hand, squeezed it a little and whispered to him,

"Give him time,"

Shaka smiled as he slowly reached for his glass with a trembling hand and took a sip.

"Trice, would you mind switching seats with me," Philia asked with a soft smile,

"Of course," Leatrice answered, moving around the table as Philia moved to sit on the other side of her uncle.

"I just wanted to be closer to you," The young woman said gently as she sat down, taking the old man's hand on the table, "I know this is hard," She continued as Jean looked at her, "But it is better to get out, so you can start to heal," She smiled weakly.

Jean nodded his head as he continued.

"How?" Diana asked, almost standing up from her seat.

Diana had never heard of something like that before. Ceres could tell that her mother was shaken at the other end of the table. Jean stood from the table and walked to one of the floor-to-ceiling windows.

"Well, this Book I'm talking about has a symbiotic relationship with its owner. We didn't know about it, which Maria had tried to warn us about so long ago. The owner benefits from it by using its knowledge to help others, and as they do so, good fortune flows naturally."

The three Bastille women shook their heads in agreement. Jean turned from the window to look at the table.

Diana sat quietly, thinking about what Jean was saying. If Esperanza had been a Priestess who never went through initiation, her link to the ancestors wouldn't be complete. To force a soul through a body not deemed worthy would require the payment of another soul. Mateo for Esperanza, Diana realized that this break in the lineage kept Esperanza trapped and the Book from seeking Philia.

'we're in more trouble than we thought,' her Spirit advised.

During those last few months, when she could still talk, Zaza had our house inscribed with sigils for protection. Then, as if she knew," Jean swallowed hard, "and with her last breath, before slipping into a coma, she made me promise to keep you, Mateo, and The Book safe until I could give it to you," He looked at Philia then took another breath and started strolling towards Shaka.

"It was not until her deathbed, Shaka, that they mentioned your name. It was before I knew you and before our friendship had come to mean so much to me,"

"You worked with them," Philia spoke dryly with contempt.

"Yes, I did, and I'm ashamed to say I even hired Shaka under pretenses just so I could get a sample of his blood for them." Jean softly patted the big man on the shoulder while Shaka's jaws tightened, and he fought the urge to get up.

Throughout the ordeal, Diana kept hold of his hand.

"I didn't even see what was right before me," Jean said. "Esperanza had always been there to point out the connective details of things to me. I was so blinded by anger and loss I didn't even notice that the cover of the book you wrote was identical to the symbol from The Book I had seen in the apothecary's shop many years ago. By the time I pieced it all together, it was too late. I finally realized how much I had lost."

"Jean, where's Esperanza's Book?" Diana asked plainly, letting go of Shaka's hand and standing directly before the older man.

"It's with the Sons of Eve,"

"Where are the Sons of Eve?"

"Everywhere, but nowhere I have access to,"

"Everywhere," Diana repeated fearfully, wondering if they had followed Jean and Shaka to her home.

"What does that mean?" Shaka asked through gritted teeth.

"They are your politicians, your business tycoons, captains of industries, Cardinals, Priests, maybe even the Pope. They're men who can trace their bloodline to Adam and Eve and the wealthy men that want to be part of it."

Shaka rolled his eyes and hissed.

"Oh, but you're not of Eve's bloodline?"

Jean ignored him.

Maggie was about to ask a question when the sound of Philia's chair sliding over the wooded floors made everyone look her way. Getting up slowly, she placed her napkin on the table and took a deep breath before walking over to her uncle to stand between him and Diana. The older Priestess moved to allow Philia space.

"Why do they want The Books?"

"I don't know," Jean answered softly. His eyes looked sad but honest.

Philia took a deep breath, closed her eyes, and asked her uncle the question again.

"Why do they want The Books?"

Shaka looked up and saw something familiar in Philia's eyes and how she stood. Philia positioned her right hand on Jean's shoulder close to his neck. Shaka nodded his understanding of what was about to happen and moved his chair into position to help the old man when he fell to his knees. However, there were no visions when Philia placed her right hand on Jean's neck.

Jean's eyes went blank. Then Jean went into a monologue. Spoke as if repeating something he had heard somebody say or had been told. His words were unsettling, even more so because of the monotone tone of his voice.

"We are here to prevent the knowledge in The Books from getting to the masses. We were late in understanding the Spiritual power of the dark continent we have benefited so well from for generations. While we focus on assimilating the men and women of this Earth to see the truth of God's law. Men were given dominion over all things, whether occult, plants, or lower animals, and women were men's supporters and caregivers.

"Why not destroy The Books?" Philia questioned, looking into her uncle's blank eyes.

Before Jean could answer the question, a feeling came over Ceres. Then, quietly, walked away from the table and went upstairs.

Philia took a deep breath and brought her hand down, taking a step. Diana stepped forward, holding her by the shoulder as Philia shook her head, trying to clear it. The older Priestess escorted her over to the couch and took a seat. Jean was still standing there, a little shaken and disoriented, as he rubbed the back of his neck.

"What was that?" He asked shakily. "I didn't know I knew all of that."

"Probably not consciously," Maggie shrugged, "We pick up information all day through our proximity to people. We overhear things like their desires, emotions, habitual thoughts, or conversations. Our minds take in everything, noticeable or not, and then we process that information differently. You have dreams, sudden eureka moments, and empathic emotional responses. You knew things you didn't know. You knew. She just helped you open yourself up to remembering the information you'd previously processed, like Hypnosis, maybe," Magalie finished thinking about that last part comparison herself.

"I see," Jean replied softly, sitting across from his niece.

"No, you don't."

Everyone turned to see Ceres looking down at them from the second-floor balcony. Her eyes were pure emerald green with a reflection of gold from the setting sun. She slowly descended the stairs, her bare feet not sounding on the wood as she held The Book to her chest.

"Domination, control, greed—such are the ways of most men." Finally, Ceres reached the first floor, and the group lost sight of her as she came around the load-bearing column in the back of the kitchen. Still, Ceres' voice could be heard.

"The Sons of Eve is a new name for an old bias," The young woman continued, "Some men will forever refuse to accept that women and men were created equal. Next to each other, side by side. They will always deny that there was Lilith, Adam's partner and equal before Eve. It was his unwillingness to see her intelligence," She continued walking in from the kitchen,

"As equal in importance as his strength — which caused her to leave him. Even though Lilith loved Adam deeply. She was carrying his children. They hold on to Eve because their mother was created to be subjugated; therefore, they believe all women should be.

As if she, too, had not learned the pain of what it was like to be subjugated by Adam. After she ate the fruit of the knowledge of good and evil. Adam left Eve alone in the wilderness on the brink of giving birth. As he went to do his 40-day penance. Only to return and watch her give birth to their first son while enduring excruciating pain. A son whose cold heart was only matched by his father's need for control named Cain."

She placed her family's Book open to a passage on the living room table for Jean to see, she sat down next to it and stared into his eyes.

"It was never supposed to be like this," Ceres continued, pointing down the open pages while placing her hand on Jean's shoulders. He felt a warmth traveling down his body as he slowly turned to look at The Book, his face coming to life as he picked it up and stared.

"Oh, mon Dieu, I can see, I can see the words!" He exclaimed.

"It was through trickery and ignorance that God's real law of equality had been siphoned for all this time," She continued. While Jean was reading the story in The Book, he was also experiencing it internally in whispers of emotions and visions.

"Angels that had been angered by Lilith's imprudence. The gall she would speak God's holy name and free herself tricked her into using her free will to bind herself and her descendants into a deal. It forbade them from freeing themselves from subjugation."

Ceres released Jean's shoulder, taking The Book and placing it back on the table before any mentions of the celestial events came up as she continued to speak.

Chapter LV - *Rose*

Roses can be used as a flower remedy and essential oil in tinctures, glycerites, teas, honey, oxymels, syrups, vinegar, and hydrosols. It's nutrient-rich, astringent, diuretic, and anti-inflammatory and also used for uplifting the spirits, grief, PMS, upset tummy, sore throats, colds, and during menopause.

In Spiritual Work: *Make a rose petal tea to boost sexuality and as an anti-inflammatory. Use candles to attract love. Burn rose petals and use the ashes to cut ties with a former lover. Add to a sachet for sleep to promote sweet dreams.*

"Throughout time, we—the daughters of Lilith—have fought their need for dominance with balance. The presence of a Reader in each generation. Keeps the information flowing to all daughters of the first woman or anyone else. We seek true wisdom, the balance of life and nature on this Earth."

As Ceres spoke, Diana watched her daughter's calm, blueish aura and smile. The Priestess understood at the moment. It was Erzulie *Granne*, the wise, mature, kind grandmother Spirit Ceres was being guided by.

Shaka had moved to sit next to Jean on the sofa and tentatively picked up The Book off the table. Shaka looked up to see if he would be stopped. Ceres didn't move. He said a silent thank you as he sat back, rotating The Book, to examine it.

"We don't seek dominance, only balance." Ceres continued

****

Shaka was only half listening to her as he tried to contain himself. After so many years of searching for his family's Book. Only now to learn there were several. He was finally holding one in his hands. Gently, he stroked the leather cover, debossed with a glyph of an ornamented heart and staff on a mortar and pestle.

He had to admit he was a little disappointed. Despite its age and apparent heft, the Book was lighter than he expected. It could have been passed off or be easily mistaken for any old reference book.

Where was the magic? He thought as he flipped the cover open.

The sense of calm that overcame Shaka was almost immediate. At first, he felt a percolating surge of warmness flowing from The Book up his finger through his arm. Until it enveloped his whole body while the pages started moving independently.

The big man stood suddenly. Ceres stopped mid-sentence. Every head at the table turned as he began to read aloud,

"On the first of the Tetra, they will be reborn, angels to initiate Spiritual freedom. Women with the alchemy of Djinns, intellect, beauty, and reasoning of their kin.

Ceres and Diana stood and walked over to Shaka as he continued reading.

"Priestesses here to educate the world, with no need, for money or kingdom. Those of old, with no care for the truth, will fear their divine knowledge, calling their teachings cancerous pustules. Four will stand, and Four will fall, four Books, for Four Priestesses, to fight the darkness and free all."

Ceres was the first to retrieve The Book from Shaka once he stopped speaking, giving up without hesitation. As he regained complete control of his faculties.

"What was that all about?" Magalie asked, taking The Book from her sister.

"I don't know. It's something written by Marie-Louise Pierrot, a granddaughter of Cécile Fatiman. She had The Book for a concise while before Erzulie gave Its charge to us," Diana replied since she had been looking over Ceres' shoulder before Magalie snatched it.

"I've never seen it before," Ceres confessed thoughtfully.

"Isn't today the last day of the Tetrad? Technically, earlier this morning, last night-ish," Philia advised, "Is that all of it?"

"What tetrad, what are you talking about?" Magalie asked, walking towards Philia with The Book.

Philia leaned over and scanned the writing, which looked like it had been done using a quill pen.

"Right there, it's like the first line," She answered, pointing out the word to Magalie with her pinky,

Magalie reread the line out loud,

*"On the first of the Tetra, they will be reborn, angels to initiate Spiritual freedom. Okay, but w*hat's a tetrad," Magalie asked.

Ceres and Diana replay the early morning event in their minds.

Philia looked at Maggie quizzically,

"It's a set of four lunar eclipses in sequence. This particular set just happened to coincide with many old Hebrew Sacred holidays. The last in the sequence of lunar eclipses started last night, ending around two, with today being the Hebrew holiday Sukkot, The Feast of Tabernacles. Don't you guys watch TV? This pastor was talking about it's the end of days and everything," She chuckled.

"Not so much," Magalie admitted, suddenly not wanting to possess The Book and giving it back to her sister.

"We spend a lot of time out of the house, doing things," Ceres confirmed, instantly finding the page.

"Well, lucky you," Philia said softly, "All I have is work and the TV to put me to sleep when I get home," She chuckled dryly.

"Oh, Philia," Jean moaned across from her.

"It kind of answers why the Sons of Eve are searching for The Books more hastily now," Diana responded.

"It appears so," confirmed Maggie, sitting next to Philia.

"On the first of the Tetra, she will be reborn," Shaka mumbled to himself. "Philia, do you know the date of the first eclipse?"

"Actually, yes, it was my birthday, April 15, last year," She admitted shyly.

A shiver ran down Diana's spine as all the Bastille women looked at her quietly.

"Which birthday was it, Cherie?"

"My twenty-second," She answered with a shrug, "It was a Monday, so we didn't do much,"

"You didn't tell me?" Shaka responded with regret as Jean sucked his teeth.

"You guys were busy with something, and I wasn't feeling well, but we did go to Rome that weekend, remember?"

"Oh, yes," Jean confirmed as Shaka nodded.

"Anyways, part of this current end-of-the-world prophecy was about the holidays. The eclipses fell on. The first," Philia continued, "On Passover, the celebration of freedom, an angel came to help celebrate freedom."

"Four Books, Four Priestesses," Ceres repeated. "Mother..."

"Four will rise, four will fall," Diana continued, cutting off her daughter. "If the prophecy is for this generation, your generation, then binding your wife to The Book," She walked over to face Jean, "Keeps Philia from assuming possession of her family's Book. That cuts us from a lot of information we need right now. We need to find that Book!"

Jean saw the anger in the woman's eyes in front of him and put his head down in shame.

"I truly wish I knew," He advised regretfully.

The tension in the room was reaching a dangerous level when Roger Taylor's voice rang out, singing in his high pitch, *Galileo...Galileo*, four women, turned to look at Leatrice sitting down on the loveseat next to Diana. However, Leatrice shrugged and shook her head.

"Sorry," Philia called out as she jumped, running for the phone in her purse on the counter.

"Seriously?" Maggie asked, looking at Ceres.

"Birds of a feather," Ceres joked with a half-smile.

"Oh, My God, Teo, we have a lot to talk about," Philia started walking toward the middle of the group where she had been previously sitting, "I have to put you on speaker, but fair warning, your dad is here," She pushed the speaker button before he could decline.

"*I don't want to talk to him, Phil,*" Mateo said on the other end, "Did you find anything in The Book?"

"No, it's gone, but."

"What do you mean, it's gone?! My father's friends, he must have given it to them!"

"N..." Jean opened his mouth to speak, but Diana placed a hand on his shoulder, quieting him down,

"It's a lot more complicated," Philia attempted to speak over Mateo, but he kept going,

"Just try to keep him away until we figure this out. I made it to The Village of Ayizan about 8 hours ago. Philia, this place is incredible. I can see why they fear what knowledge might be in our Book. The Spiritual Leader advised me that even if I had possession of The Book, which she knew I didn't," Mateo laughed dryly,

"It would be useless to us as it is right now, so whatever Dad's pals did after they stole it is fucked up," Mateo laughed again.

"You need to come here, you and two sisters. I'm unsure who the other two women the Priestess is talking about. She's sure you know; however, you must get here before the next moon. I can't stay on the phone long but get to Benin, the hotel, and Azalai. They will be expecting you at the desk, and from there, you will find your way to me,"

"Mateo, that's not a lot to go on, and you need to know there are dangerous people after you, so you need to be careful," Philia hurried to get out the sentence.

"Philia, right now, I promise you, I'm probably in the safest place on Earth from these people. What I do need is for you and whoever these sisters are to get here now. There are better directions on how to find this place. Just get to the Azalai Hotel in Cotonou, Benin."

"Okay, we will leave right away."

"I'll see you soon. I have to go; I want to speak more to the Priestess. Before she heads back to her sanctuary. I love you; be careful over there by yourself."

"Love you too, Teo," Philia managed to finish before the call ended.

"Benin?" Magalie questioned with a sour face.

"Many of the slaves from Haiti came from Benin," Leatrice informed the group, "It's where Vodou originates from."

"I guess we're heading East," Diana said firmly.

"No," Gerda corrected softly, reaching over to take hold of her friend's hand from her seat by Leatrice,

"They need to go to Benin, and from what we heard, only them," Gerda finished, squeezing Diana's hand reassuringly.

Epilogue

"Welcome to Ayizan Velekete Village," Malik informed him.

Mateo paused with wonder as he placed his bag down to fully appreciate what he was seeing.

The Village of Velekete lay in the bowl-shaped valley about 200' before them. Nestled into the protective arms of an extensive range of green mountains. Which reached thousands of feet into the sky. The homes were modern with an angular design that reminded Mateo of the architect *Stemmer Rodrigues*. They were painted white with dark opaque roofs that glimmered through tall fruit trees, with each house separated from its neighbor by bright flower hedges. They lined up in twelve neatly laid out, half-moon-like semi-circles, 6 rows to the North and 6 to the South. All face a majestically twinkling dome floating in the center of a blue-green lake.

"Wow," Mateo exclaimed as he took a few steps to better see the village that looked like a large eye gazing towards heaven.

Mateo studied the artificial-colored walkway they were standing on. It ran around the perimeter, defining its shape like a light brown eyeliner. The eye split into four quadrants by paths that ran North to South and East to West, widening as they spiraled outward to two enormous metal gates behind them. The gates were attached with silver hinges the size of 1950s mini coopers, seemingly fused into the rock formations. The small door they had entered through was on the left of one of the gates. Next to that stood a small reflective glass security station.

Mateo looked up to admire the fortitude of the barrier but reflexively took a step back as he saw the symbol painted in white, split in half by the solid doors. He unconsciously touched the silver pendant around his neck, a gift from his mother on his twenty-second birthday. Esperanza had been very sick even then, yet she had found hidden strength to celebrate that birthday with her family.

'*Twenty-two is a special birthday,*' *She had told Mateo with a smile and teary eyes, 'it is when the full power of our energy emerges, disorganized and chaotic. This is when your mettle will be tested the most, something I wished I had known at that age before I ran away with your father.*'

The forbidden history continues in Book 4.

About the author

Luna Charles, is a Haitian-American writer who has authored numerous books, articles, and essays. Besides being an accomplished author, Luna is also a dedicated student of Theology, Metaphysics, and Philosophy. As a mother of two lovely girls, Luna has spent most of her life in South Florida.